Author Vanessa Wrixon

CW00383561

Book Title Haunted

© 2022

Self-published

(devilvness@yahoo.co.uk)

All rights reserved.

Copyright page

Thank you for buying my book. Hope you enjoy reading it

Vanessa

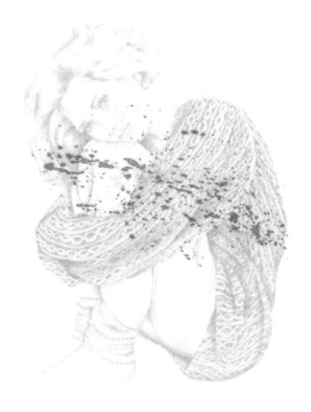

The ghost realm is as real as this one.
Reality is only real when you're in it.

CHAPTER 1

As we drove closer to my shack, I couldn't help but smile to myself. I have learnt so many lessons in love, I have listened, felt and sensed all the emotions love can bring and because of these simple actions, love has changed my life forever.

Of course this is only just the beginning, but I am convinced that with a new positivity in my life, it looks as if I will experience an exhilarating, exciting and passionate ride, possibly with a hint of danger thrown in for good measure. At last I am so content to be Mrs Meyers and enjoy life as a couple.

I relaxed back onto the head rest and stared at Tim, feeling my smile grow of its own accord, now I can either let him see what he has ignited or hide it, either way, he's the most fun and best thing in my world. I started to let my eyes do the dreaming, whilst my brain weaved an array of erotic fantasies. I sighed softly, as if the switch from reaction to reflection, was ready to arrive at a good response.

My erotism was short lived as Tim brought me back to reality, stealing a quick glance in my direction. "Darling, just need to do a quick detour, if that's ok?" Tim winked, "Sure no probs," came my lovesick reply, he blows my mind with command and I'm putty in his hands, for the first time in my life I had no concrete plans at all, apart from being with him. Those eyes, that voice, that electric touch and sexy confidence renders me completely incoherent. I know, I know, I have it bad, but for me, all that matters right here and now is that we are together forever and so very much in love.

We were driving back from Robert L. Bradshaw Airport on the Island of St Kitts where we had landed, disembarked and picked up Tim's car only half an hour ago after the most fantastic honeymoon. The Island is not very big, so it doesn't take long to drive anywhere, even with some of the roads being in a complete state of disrepair, you just need to watch out for the ever growing potholes! Thankfully my shack was on a reasonably good route, after campaigning through the Alise to get a few of the roads repaired.

It happened as a result of my car getting seriously stuck in a pothole a year or so ago, it made me late for an appointment and trashed my wheel and axle, not to mention the amount of time it took a hoard of locals to extract my car. So there comes a time when "pushing" one's ideas to help our Island becomes morally the right thing to do. The Alise published a spread on how the government's job isn't to keep election promises, but to bow to the "money" keep us working, paying tax for no benefits at all. We wrote that they were corrupted even before the ballots were cast, too bamboozled with lobbyists and dazzled by greed to see daylight let alone the "bigger picture." Well, we are supposed to live in a democracy, funny how quickly things got sorted!

Anyway, I digress, all I really wanted to do was get home, have a cup of tea and enjoy each other, how typically English despite living in the Caribbean for nearly five years, there are some traits you can never give up! Now I will have to wait a bit longer with this new detour coming to light, something to do with his job I expect, he was like a battery, charged and ever ready!

For our honeymoon we could have chosen to travel anywhere in the world I suppose, yet all we wanted was to enjoy some soulful time with each other, without having to venture too far, relaxing after our whirlwind romance and subsequent wedding. We decided to 'Island hop,' as they call, it along the Caribbean coast, visiting different towns and villages, absolutely no planned agenda just stopping wherever we wanted.

We found some great quirky hotels to rest our heads for the night before we moved on, everybody was so friendly and eager to please. Some days we decided to stay in one place for longer, exploring the area a little deeper, soaking up the atmosphere and sights. At one of the larger towns on our trip, we came across an outdoor Jacuzzi garden with massage rooms and a Japanese bath, all in low-lying pavilions overlooking the sea, so we indulged in a pampering session, quite erotic I must say, the seduction happened before we even uttered a word, our souls in complete recognition of one another. Everything else that followed was a divine dance towards the release of sweet passions, the kind that would ensure our destinies were meant to be.

However our favourite time of all was when it was just the two of us, I am sure there is a song that starts like that! Anyway what I mean is, when there was no one else around, just us amid the beautiful scenery, sitting in the summer brightness on the hilltops looking at the towns below laid out like living maps, feeling the gentle breeze that was the only relief from the heat of the day. Quite often our desires would get the better of us, but then we were on honeymoon, so we could be excused.

I remember on one occasion, I was astride Tim, my dress riding up my thighs, all done in one fluid motion. I was much better at seduction these days, moving into Tims's personal space with just the right look of heat in my eyes. I didn't just look at my man, but looked into him knowing his primal desires. With every one of my kisses came the smooth touch of my body, poised, just the right blend of relaxation and tension, nothing was spoken between us, millions of years of evolution had already taken care of any messages.

As Tim continued to detour, I carried on reminiscing about our wedding day, it seems so long ago now. It was an unusual wedding here on the Island. My parents flew over and seemed to really enjoy themselves, they appeared to all the world full of pride, radiant, so proud of me.

Our wedding was simple, our vows taken under a pergola woven with a vibrant reddy orange bloom from the flame vine in the botanical gardens. I don't enjoy being the centre of attention and find it completely unnecessary and vulgar to spend lots of money when you don't need to. Despite its simplicity, it was the best day ever. What had only been an expanse of green foliage the previous week became a garland of the most vibrant blooms for our day, colours to weave dreams from. A compendium of the birds sang their songs, adorning the sky with their rich emotional music, turning it into gentle airwaves. The trees arched into the bluest of skies, their shadows played all day with the sunlight, turning it into differing hues, promising to be the canvas to laughter and a few happy tears. It was just perfect, my fairytale wedding.

We both wanted to steer away from any egotistical traditions and instead go for things that felt so much more heart-warming and sweet. So aside from Tim and I, everyone dressed in their Sunday best, "No new outfits" was the order of the day. My wedding dress was my mothers, altered slightly to fit the modern day. Ice-white satin with a fitted, boat-necked bodice, short sleeves embellished with tiny buttons, and full circular skirt with a demi-train that swept the floor. Tim wore his best business suit, which was as crisp as a new banknote, it showed off his sexy muscular physique to perfection.

As I said, it was an amazing day, all the sweeter for its informality and the focus on our love, we both wanted to tell any children we may have in the future that we started this marriage on the right foot, so very much in love with one another and at one with nature. Our wedding reception was a simple garden party, lots of food and drink, each dish made from scratch by our guests. There was so much love in the air it was as if a new kind of electricity had been rekindled, so palpable and real amid the flowers, a romantic hue, I think everyone there was renewed that day.

To also break from the norm, instead of the usual gifts that we all have too many of already, our guests were asked to bring something homemade, create something from the craft world that best described Tim and I. Slightly tricky if you didn't know us that well. I have to say, I'm not sure that it was the best idea we have ever had, when I think back to some of the oddities we were given. I don't mean to sound ungrateful, at least the thought was there. Goldie of course, excelled by having individual photos of herself, Leroy, Tim and I printed onto cloth and then turning the cloth into a grotesque table cover with four matching seat cushions. She announced that she was going to make matching curtains but she ran out of time. Thank God for that! They say everyone has a bottom drawer and that is exactly where that gift will go!

As I glanced out of the window, we turned a sharp corner and continued up and around a circular driveway, that was somewhat overgrown, but despite that, the fauna and flora helped it to take on an almost meditative quality, with the sunlight igniting the hues bursting through the trees. This place had a vague familiarity to it.

I shivered as a chill ran through me, then it hit me, oh my God, no surely not, what were we doing here? I definitely recognised it now. We pulled up outside the front of the mansion and Tim helped me out of the car. "Here we are then." Was all he said sweeping both arms outwards to show the mansion looming in front of us, and wearing a grin as big as a cheshire cats on his face. The mansion had long loved the land, its demeanour carrying the memory of its creation long ago. Despite being back here, weirdly I felt a sense of belonging.

CHAPTER 2

The rocky steps that had been laid with loving care to last the ages, were looking a little more rickety now with the weathering of seasons. But I suppose that just added to their beauty as they stood before our very eyes. The soft undulations on the stones amongst the weeds told the passage of centuries, of soles trodden upon it as it dreamily swept the way to the doors.

As I looked up past the steps towards the entrance, the two large overpowering teak doors still firmly stood, slightly weathered in colour by the onslaught of the sun, they were still held up by the same ostentatious pillars that I remember from my previous visit. A proud invitation to a possible new adventure, a new challenge, maybe it was fate, but for some unknown reason, which I am sure will become clear very soon, I was back here, some five years later, give or take a few months, trying very hard not to let my quashed nightmares surface again.

For those of you that haven't guessed already, it was of course Iberville, the sugar plantation where my life changed for ever, some bad, some good. I suppose the only way to find out odd experience would become was to reach out, open it and step in, but something was stopping me. If I think about it rationally and maybe if the events leading up to this day hadn't happened, probability says that I wouldn't have become Editor of the Alise newspaper or met and married Tim, but there was one question I couldn't answer; why on earth had he brought me back here now? He knew all about what had happened here, there were very few secrets between us.

I stood rooted to the spot, staring inanely ahead, trying to take it all in. Over thinking it all caused a sudden wave of panic to take hold and try to grow stronger. I felt like a child again, shaking, terrified, reverting to my inner self as if I was being smothered by the air about me. The only resolution to my conflicted thoughts, was an inside job that requires my brain to gain control and have all my bad memories rescinded. Tim must have sensed my anxieties, he took hold of my hand, squeezed it tightly and then kissed me softly. In that moment I felt my body begin to relax, I was after all in his protective cocoon, he would never let anything happen to me, he had already proved that many a time.

This still doesn't bring me any closer to understanding why I am standing in front of Iberville with Tim having no immediate urge to enlighten me at this moment in time. So I will give you some insight as to past events (and two previous books) whilst I try to fathom it out.

I arrived here in the Caribbean nearly five years ago now, gosh where does the time go? Initially my first job was working as a junior Journalist for a small online paper in Henley, Sussex, England. My boss at the time luckily saw the potential in me and helped to land me a job full of more opportunities at the Alise newspaper in St Kitts and Nevis. Since then I have excelled at my work and climbed the promotional ladder, rising to the role of Editor, or 'The Boss' as my staff affectionately call me. I started my life here in a little shack which I managed to buy with some money mum and dad gave me, it is still my home, my sanctuary, but about to become our home. Tim and I decided to live there for now until we find something we both like and can put our own mark on.

I absolutely love it here in the Caribbean, the scenery, the beaches, the warm weather, although I do miss the changing seasons of good old Blighty! The people here are so friendly and despite it taking a bit of getting used to, I have come to enjoy the laid back lifestyle, 'limin,' as they call it, which is why I have made the Island my permanent home.

Anyway it wasn't long after arriving on St Kitts and Nevis, that a local fisherman named Blot was out catching his daily supply of bait to sell on, when he netted a woman's body. It just happened to occur on the beach which my shack overlooked. So I got involved, at the time I thought it would be a great spread for the newspaper. I helped Blot haul her onto the beach, as none of the gathered locals were going to get their feet wet! Then tried my hand at a spot of investigatatory work, if I could solve her death, imagine what it would do for my ego and it would put the Alise newspaper on an even higher pedestal. I could just visualise the headlines at the time. "Is no woman safe from villainous murders," case solved by Jasmine Tormolis, Senior Reporter of the Alise.

Unfortunately, it didn't pan out that way due to Police corruption at the time. The philosophy of money here corrupts society, making a cold indifference, a survival advantage if you like, so corruption became a sort of sport in which all the medals were gold. I have to say it is slightly improved these days, with new reforms brought in. Policing on the Island today has begun to attract a different kind of person, more committed to social healing and keeping our communities safe.

Anyway, at the time, I was warned off by various parties which I later found out to my detriment, all had some part to play in the murder of the woman. Being the enthusiastic reporter I was at the time, I ignored all the warnings and tell tale signs which should have led me to back off and instead continued to dig deeper to unearth the truth. When I look back now, I was quite gullible, I would have never expected my then sub-editor and line manager Tilly Colspur to be in cahoots with the local dignitary Lord Wrexham or more to the point, find that the two of them plotted together and committed the murder of his wife, Lady Amélie Wrexham, whose body was netted by Blot. Well, you wouldn't would you?

Tilly needed to silence me, after all the last thing she needed was for the Islanders to find out about her romantic affair with Lord Wrexham and their plot to murder Lady Amélie Wrexham. Tilly blackmailed two of my close friends, as a sort of psychological control and then had me kidnapped, holding me hostage until my two friends managed to find a way to free me and spill the beans on what was going on. Unfortunately they paid the ultimate price, both of them lost their lives as a result.

I still really miss Candice and Winston and think of them often, but as the years have past it has got easier. I won't ever forget them and I often find myself wondering what they are up to in that big world in the sky, knowing Candice as I did, she would be getting herself into all sorts of scrapes, probably managing to coerce gentle natured Winston in the process.

With the valued support of my now best friend and colleague Goldie and my previous Alise boss Petra, the authorities managed to track down and eventually catch Tilly and Ed who were imprisoned for life. Well, thats what we all thought, however, their captivity was short lived as they managed to use Ed's notoriety as an aid to their escape.

Somehow Ed got word to an American gang-lord, who had an urge to become a superhero and make victories possible that otherwise would never have been. So Ed and Tilly escaped and began a new life elsewhere, becoming wrapped up in drug trafficking and gun running. They managed to evade all authorities at every turn, being one step ahead.

So enter Tim and Leroy, two secret agents that were enlisted and released into the field to flush them out and aid their capture once and for all. This is how I met Tim, he did his research, found out all about me and what had happened. He set up a fake website pretending to be an editor for a newspaper in Anegada, inviting me and one of my best reporters, who happened to be Goldie, to travel to the Island for an all expenses paid holiday and to write a spread in the Alise to promote Anegada within the tourism industry. Leroy was the ears and eyes on the ground, working alongside Tim as an undercover bartender. Basically it was all a lie, a complete set up, we were lured there as bait to help flush out Tilly and Ed as we later found out, when we became deeply embroiled with the two of them.

CHAPTER 3

To cut a very long story short, nearly five years on (and as I said two books later) Tilly and Ed were flushed out into the open by yours truly with Goldie, Tim and Leroy.

Unfortunately, or fortunately depending on how you look at it, Ed met his demise in a diving accident, in which he nearly succeeded in killing me, but Leroy came to my rescue and at worst I landed myself an overnight stay in hospital. This wasn't to be the end as a hostile Tilly came after us, seeking revenge for her beloved Ed's untimely death.

She decided to forgo her life as a fugitive and tried to attack us whilst we were kite surfing, in her eyes we would be at our most vulnerable. If she was watching us at the time it would have been very clear, even to the untrained eye, that we were new to this. Again things didn't go her way and she was caught out by strong tidal currents. Despite frantic efforts by Tim and Leroy to save Tilly, they were unable to reach her, the waves changed and became like a coiffured fifties hair do, over pronounced in their formation. We watched on helpless, impossible to avert our gaze, as she took a last breath and disappeared beneath the waves for the last time, never to be seen or heard of again.

A few days later, I unexpectedly received a text message from an anonymous number, it was Tilly, saying she was sorry and begging me to help her, she wanted her soul to be saved and begin a new life, even if that meant a life behind bars. How she had got and used my mobile number, I still have no ideas to this day. Despite my concerns that she was actually still alive and would come after us, nothing has been seen or heard of her since we left Anegada. Tim remains convinced that it was all just a ruse and is still adamant to this day that she is dead.

As a result of our Anegada trip, Tim's colleague Leroy, 'got it together' so to speak with Goldie and they are now also married, they tied the knot in an ornate wedding ceremony a few weeks before us. Tim and I have always been a bit slower off the mark, but eventually despite a cautious beginning, more so on my part, we fell head over heels for one another in a whirlwind romance.

Back to the present day, as the boss at the Alise, I head a good team and we churn out some fantastic stories, but to be honest, I really don't enjoy it anymore, I want that, 'je ne say quoi.' Goldie keeps me sane and ensures my feet are firmly on the ground in work as well as out, she is my right hand person and best friend. Since returning from her honeymoon, she and her new husband Leroy are living in her rented accommodation next door to the Alise, but that is only for the very short term as they look for a place to make their own, much the same as Tim and I.

Well, that brief synopsis brings things more or less up to speed (but you will have to read Iberville and Temptation, my previous books if you want to learn more of my in-depth encounters, I am not about to give away all that has happened now am I!).

Despite my rambling and time to think, none of it has bought me any closer as to why I am stood here still staring at Iberville. Tim who has been very patient up to now, wrapped his strong arms around me, his way of letting me know everything is all right. He is my human shield and in our moments of togetherness, I always feel that we are at the centre of our own divine vortex. He kissed me again, this time on the forehead, "Earth to Jaz, come in," he uttered smiling at me, "home sweet home, what do you think?" I gave him one of my weird, what the hell looks, completely shocked and bewildered but at the same time needing some more clarity on what I think I had just heard pass his lips. "Wwwhat, I beg your pardon, what did you just say?" I stuttered. "Home sweet home," he repeated. I thought that is what I heard, I am now at a complete loss for words, my brain still desperately trying to process the enormity of what Tim had just said.

I can't really explain how or what I feel at this moment in time. Numb possibly, no more than that, there is a silence in my heart, a chill in my blood, coldness bringing the synapses of my brain to a stand still. A sort of pain I have to endure. I find it difficult when negative emotions and opinions from the past and present come in thick and fast all at once. I revert to the kind of internal communication mankind used before we learned to speak, a type of emotional processing. I can feel the emotions but can't say the words until I eventually release it with an outburst in the form of a cross word or just plain old tears.

Tim held me close and hugged me even tighter as if I was his teddy and he was enjoying squeezing the stuffing out of me, in that embrace the world stopped still on its axis. There was no time, no wind and no rain, my mind felt at peace, how could it not be, Tim was pure, unselfish, undemanding, my protector from evil. I could feel my body being pressed into him, he was so soft and warm. This was my emotional rescue, made all the more effective and longer lasting with a real sense of comfort.

As I snuggled into Tim even more, I really wanted my emotions to blend with his in the most delicious of ways. I wanted us to have that special something that will steer us down the right paths together to a new and beautiful vista. But it's these storms from Iberville that trigger negative thoughts and still haunt, I need to learn how to forget them completely and see Tim through the lens of his needs and emotions rather than simply my own selfish needs, we are a couple now, I need to be generous with my perspective, grow and mature more, so that I can become capable of better choices that will help both of us. I need to use my emotional intelligence to see with a clearer vision and help make the future perfect for us, after all I can't change the past.

I pulled back from our embrace slightly and looked up at him, a million thoughts still careering through my mind. He looked so awkward and forlorn, to break the deathly silence he uttered, "Jaz, sweetheart are you ok? I hope I haven't hurt you, I bought Iberville for us, a castle for my beautiful princess. I thought you might like it. I know it has a past with you, but I can help you overcome that, conquer your fears, we can do it up however we want, change things and lay those demons of yours to rest once and for all. I want everything to be perfect for you, for us." I nodded as he smirked, "You said you want another job, well you could turn your hand to ghost hunting, put Lady Amélie's soul to rest, some say she still wonders the rooms here, what do you say?"

He laughed nervously, this was the first time that I sensed an unsettling feeling begin to well inside him, completely unsure that he had done the right thing. I wish right now I could tell him that all would be ok, but at this moment in time, I really wasn't sure of that myself.

After an awkward pause, I managed to regain control of my thoughts, relax a bit more and let my lips stretch into small smile, don't get me wrong it was still the kind of smile that said I was scared and uncomfortable, but it was a start. "Jaz, say something, please, I am so sorry if I have done the wrong thing, you mean the world to me, I never meant to hurt you, if it's not what you want we can live in your shack for now until we decide what to do." He was so understanding but his voice was faltering and his eyes told of a different story, he looked so sad, he really wants to make me happy to make it perfect for us.

Hesitation is a natural thing, the best of hearts are cautious and the best of hearts say things we all need to listen to and take note of, all good things are worth waiting for, right? So having had time to think about this, I have decided to let the happiness soak through me as I savoured the moment for just a minute longer.

I looked at his lips and stretched up, it is the feel of them that sends my mind into a sensual state of intoxication. I touched them lightly before the urge to kiss him took over and in that moment our chemistry became that ever-bright flame.

It was going to be the weirdest thing for me, Mrs Jasmine Meyers nee Tormolis to have Iberville as my home. Tim and I can definitely change it, its memories and its future together. I am a firm believer that this is a prequel to whatever comes next, the old book has closed and a new one has just opened. Whatever is ahead of us will be a challenge, but it is our challenge and our adventure to take, the ideas will come, probably when we least expect it, so I am going to be positive and move forward with a strong conviction that this will turn out fine for us both.

Eventually I spoke, an inner excitement had found itself and surged to the surface. "Tim, I love you, I love it, it's amazing, thank you so much, you have done the right thing, really, you just caught me off guard thats all, I never for one moment dreamt that this would become our home, I love you so much, let's do it, let's move in." A huge exhalation of pent-up breath came from Tim as a sigh of relief. "Really?" He questioned still slightly unnerved but an excited glint in his eyes returned. "Yes, really, this is the most romantic gesture ever, let's have some fun here except for the ghost hunter bit, I am not too enamoured about that idea."

CHAPTER 4

Tim pulled me even tighter against his chest, as if he actually could, I felt like I was already having my juice squeezed out of me. He seemed relieved that I had come to this decision and began to let his hand glide erotically down my back caressing me gently, he was like the cat that got the cream. His eyes even more alight, like candles, their new light a spark of passionate desire. A small but teasing smile crept across his face, as goosebumps continued to line my skin, the kind you get when nothing else in the world matters, except right here, right now. "I love you so much, I know this is a really big decision for you, I want you and us to be so happy, but it has to feel right and be right for you." He whispered back in my ear, his gentle warm breath causing me to be putty in his hands even further.

I nodded, "I know, it's all a bit of a shock, but it will feel right," what am I saying? "it is right, it does feel the right thing to do, we can make it ours, have it just how we want it," I replied as we broke free from the embrace, locked arms and began carefully to climb the broken steps. Unbelievable, Iberville was ours, all ours, I wanted someone to pinch me, wake me up from this dream, but there was no need, this really was real, it really was happening.

We reached the top with no twisted ankles, the imposing doors for a moment intimidating. Tim turned the key in the lock and with some difficulty even for him, managed eventually to push open one of the large doors, my goodness, did it moan, groan and creak, it's only way of showing resistance at being opened I suspect. I would do the same, it's only fair, after being neglected for a few years!

Tentatively we peered inside, Tim hadn't stepped foot into the place before, he just bought it on a whim, as they say. An old dusty woven mat greeted us, fashioned from rustic strings it seemed to have adhered itself to the floor, it was still enriched with the mud left by thousands of shoes, a testimony to the lives that had once passed through here. We could almost imagine the memories it held. It should have been replaced many years ago, but it had a certain charm, its threadbare existence, frayed and curled edges could still mustered enough material to proudly welcome any visitor.

Tim handed me the key, "Go on then, you take the first step into our new home." I grinned, it sounded weird no matter how many times it was said, "our new home." I hesitated instead of moving forward, waiting patiently hoping the penny would drop and we could continue at least one tradition at the start of our married life! Tim smirked.

All over the world it remains a tradition you see, for the groom to carry his bride over the threshold of their new home, apparently it stems from some ancient belief that the female line of newlyweds are more susceptible to evil spirits, so by carrying his bride over the threshold, the groom is putting a protective space between her and the floor and in turn warding off all ghosts. My mother used to tell me that it was because it was considered ladylike to give the appearance of being unwilling to "give yourself or throw yourself" at your new husband. He had to work to keep his trophy, which is why you waited until he whisked you off your feet and through the front door. However spurious either of these superstitions were, it doesn't really matter, it was fun just to watch Tim's facial ticks as the cogs began to turn and he slowly put two and two together.

After a somewhat extended pause, hallelujah, the penny dropped. "Oh yes, sorry, Mrs Meyers, it is my honour to carry you over the threshold, climb upon my back ye wench" he uttered bending forward like some human mule, waiting for me to leap onto his back. Just as I was about to oblige, he straighten a little and pretended to mop his brow, "Phew, wait a moment, just need to steady myself, I have lifted some heavy weights in my time, but…" He laughed and luckily for him decided not to finish the sentence, instead he began laughing like a little boy, like everything was tickling him as funny, there was one idea coming from his mouth there were several more queuing up in his mind. I wasn't going to rise to it, I knew he was only joking, but laughing aside, it is not the type of thing you should ever say to any woman at anytime in her life, it can easily be misconstrued as rude and hurtful. I was quite slim and actually considered myself of a somewhat athletic build, despite the food and alcohol I had over indulged in on our honeymoon.

He regained his composure and smirked again, still waiting for me to retaliate. There was that little rise in the corner of his mouth that reappeared with a cool detachment in his eyes, this was giving him an inner delight, he was savouring every moment. I grinned back, I didn't say anything but instead, ran my hands through my hair, down over my t-shirt and down the side of my skirt accidentally lifting it up in the process, revealing a quick flash of my underwear. What a tease, but I left him wanting more that was for sure.

He wiped his brow for real this time as between us laughter echoed around. Enough was enough, we both decided to break with tradition, hold hands and jump over the threshold together, "Lets hope the evil spirits don't get us, ready one, two, three," Tim said as we toppled over each other landing on the floor amid plumes of erupting dust which was made worse by us waving our arms in front of us, in actual fact, all it did was result in a coughing fit for us both.

Finding ourselves on top of one another at this stage in our relationship would normally result in a healthy striptease and a passionate encounter, however laying amid a thick layer of dust that was more like fur and fragments of old cobwebs, with a plume of particles that would resemble a mushroom cloud of dead skin rising into the air every time we moved was not my idea of being turned on!

We stood up and dusted ourselves off, the air smelt stagnant, a festering pool of water that hadn't flowed in years. An errant shaft of daylight tried to burst through the cracks in the boarded up windows, it was the only light besides the open door to cast a glimmer of hope on the old grand entrance hall.

We stood rooted to the spot, trying to stretch our eyes as wide as possible and take in the dusty scene. There was an eeriness to the place, despite the warmth outside, inside it felt bleak and somber, cold, sinister even. A solitary brass lamp lost in the semi darkness was mounted upon the cracked wall, two thin upthrust arms extended electric candles with their tapered bulbs cast soft shadows transforming the lamp into a visage of some dark god who mocked the light. Knowing my luck there were probably many happy homes for spiders, cockroaches amid the rust, mildew and ripped curtains.

We decided to conquer the vortex of dust that came with any movement we made and took a few more steps forward. Tim pulled the teak doors even more open, letting the dusty particles reflect the sun-rays and take on the appearance of glitter, or perhaps pixie dust, rather than a dull grey sheen of fur that was stuck to everything. Dusty floors, walls, curtains, window boards and much more, there was no escape from the powdered mud that settled as it swirled through the dry air as it made its way into our lungs.

As we moved further into the great hall, I was right, those happiest of architects, the common spider had made this their home, adorning anything they could with their lacework. It stretched out as far as it the eye could see, pure strands of white fibre, woven into one of nature's beautiful structures. Little ants flowed in places as if they were in a celebration procession, taking on their task to conquer what would seem like mountainous regions to them, a pure example of dedication and team work. Just think if all jobs were performed with as much speed and co-operation as they have, how much quicker things would actually get done in real life.

Poor Iberville, it gave the perspective of the passing years in a world that had accelerated beyond sense, I could feel its history and memories echoing within its walls, but this once bold sugar plantation was now nothing more than an unwelcoming, almost macabre pile of bricks and mortar. Even some of the furniture that lay lifeless in a disorderedly pile, cluttering the floor reminded me of death and desperation.

The large cupcake chair was still there, sitting alone in a corner covered in dirt but with a few more holes where some fabric eating insect had made its nest. The visions of me falling into this chair whilst in a drunken stupor at the Iberville shindig some years ago reappeared at the fore front of my mind, what had once been a cosy, comfortable chair to fall asleep in, prior to my kidnapping, was now just a shadow of its former self, abandoned like everything else here except for the insects that had claimed Iberville as their home.

This place had no positive energy about it despite the fact it had been an integral part of many lives in the past, now it had chosen a life of solitude for itself. Perhaps in a few years it will be reborn again and enjoy the luxury of our company and its new lease of life filled with laughter. We could exfoliate the walls and more, enhance the beauty of this old place and marvel at how it has grown so much in such a short time. In the place where it had once been old floor boards could be a swimming pool, clear blue waters calm and still, we could make this work.

Peering briefly into the various doorways off the great hall, the one theme that was evolving was the amount of old newspapers strewn across the floor covered in insect debris. I bent down for a closer look, they were dated five years ago, I suppose that was the last time this house had seen anyone. Most of them had fearful headlines with doom and gloom but then right next to that were pictures of perfect cakes and happy weddings. I do think it's odd how as journalists we are able to use strong emotive words that register in peoples brains and can cause instant mood changes. When there is doom and gloom to report, people wander around with sullen faces as if a grey cloud is hanging over them, but spread a little good news and there are more smiles to be seen, people are more attentive to one another, how weird!

I became aware of a brown crate labelled "FRAGILE, do not touch," of course what happens when you see that, curiosity takes over and you look don't you? Well, I was no exception, I peered inside hoping to see something expensive and special, but all it housed was broken jars, plates, and glassware that smelt rancid, nothing of any value that I could see but probably worth something to someone back in their day.

The house creaked and moaned as we continued to move around, every surface we touched felt rough and sticky in some areas. I ran my fingers along the surface, no idea why I did that, habit I suppose, it was hardly going to be clean now was it? Anyway I raised my fingers for Tim to see, dust clinging to it in fat wads, "Dusty!" I crowed trying to put on an aristocratic voice. Tim laughed and put his hands to his mouth, as if it was a shocking surprise. "Is that as far as your acting ability goes?" He smirked.

This place was just like something out of a halloween scene, quite haunting, fingers crossed nothing would collapse on us or jump out of the semi darkness. Spooky is in the heart of the beholder, and this place has rather enjoyed its less than traditional vibe.

CHAPTER 5

Despite its derelict and abandoned state Iberville still had its hold on us, wanting us to be intrigued and to investigate further, we took a shallow breath, mainly not to inhale too much dust into our lungs and began to pull off a few more of the window boards to let the light stream in.

It did help being able to see things more clearly, it gave a different perspective, so curiosity got the better of us and we decided to explore more for a little longer. On the one hand there was so much to take in, but on the other we had just landed an hour or so ago and needed to shower, eat and sleep. We did after all have all the time in the world and the place would still be here tomorrow or the day after. It had stood in all weathers, as if there was a pride in its lasting so it wasn't going to collapse any time soon. This old ruin was just the kind of imperfection that our imagination falls in love with and begins to build and rebuild, ever seeking to honour its beginnings, how exciting!

So for a little longer we ventured from room to room, finding a couple of hidden gems, secret rooms, that we could explore on our next visit. I felt fairly confident that as we renovated this place, it would reveal even more surprises that we never knew existed. It would cost us a pretty packet that was for sure and take us an age to restore it to its former glory, but actually the longer I spent here, the more I felt a strong emotional pull to it. I did really want this to be our forever home more than anything else in the world.

I am not going to kid myself that we won't need to modernise Iberville an awful lot and in doing so it will present us with many challenges, but it will be fun, we can make this work for us, I am already beginning to get a nauseating excitement as I look around, redesigning some of the rooms, I can even paint an image of the restored result in my head.

Moving back into the hall, I noticed more cracked windows and walls, some cracks so large you could hide inside. All competing with mould, rising damp and wood rot, this was probably going to be a continuous theme throughout. I stood still momentarily mesmerised by the slivers of light, mosaic in colour trying to fight their way in from outside, ready to trespass and ignite the dusty hues and give warmth to the place. I stretched my hand upward, allowing the light to flow about my fingers as water does bringing me a warm feeling of satisfaction.

I stepped onto the spiral staircase with some anticipation, marvelling at the great heights that Iberville's ancestors had achieved over the years of yesterday. The ceiling must be at least thirty feet high, with plaster designs of fruit and flowers carved into the mouldings amid small, fat dirty children with wings that stared forlornly down at me from every angle. Family portraits and various landscapes painted in oils still hung in their frames, trying to tell a story through emotion and visual dreams, a societal medicine that drew you in to the pictures, except now not so much, they were darkened by the dirt that clung to them, so had lost their powers to impress somewhat.

The carved mahogany bannister, despite its poor state, still held onto its grandeur. I remember being impressed with its twisting perfect spiral when Lord Wrexham had addressed the gathered dignitaries and media at his open-house promotional party all those years before when the house was at its best and everyone had dressed up for the occasion. Now the wood had that sticky feel to it like the rest of the place, no longer polished or able to gleam as the shards of light bounced off of it. Tim decided to investigate through the doorway to left of the staircase, the dining room if my memory serves me right. As he left, he indicated upwards at the dirty ancient looking but most monumental chandelier, "That's definitely a keeper, we can clean it and let it regain its opulence." I said, Tim nodded in agreement, "See what else you can find." He shouted as he disappeared through the doorway of the dining room coughing as a cloud of dust erupted behind him just like he was Houdini.

I continued up the swirling staircase until I reached the top before pausing briefly, I felt slightly light-headed and breathless as I stared back down, becoming lost in the glorious spiral, each step fanning out from the centre core with exacting precision, an exuberance of the finest wood. I imaged myself as a princess, floating down the staircase, holding on to the reassuringly solid mahogany topped banister, all eyes on me as the pageantries took place, my gown would be made from blue satin with a silk overlay. I would be a delightful feast for the eye and the staircase would make its contribution to the edification of those minds whose feet choose to climb its heights. I really was getting above my station! In reality, the only thing I would be wearing for the foreseeable future was overalls and a cap at best!

To my left was a room I couldn't remember seeing on the Iberville tour, I know it had been a while but I do consider myself to have quite a good memory. The door was half off its hinges and partly leaning on the wall of the room, cautiously I peered in. The floorboards had become bowed and some were missing, yet more wood rot I assume from the exuding stale smell. I stepped in carefully making sure of my exact moves and position of my feet, I had a slightly uncomfortable feeling about this, one wrong step and I could disappear through the ceiling at any given moment, goodness only knows where I would end up, hopefully in the arms of my gorgeous husband below would be my first choice.

Phew, after holding my breath, I managed to make it to the window and prised off the wooden board, it didn't take much, it more or less fell off. The light streamed in as much as it could, the pattern of the dirt on the pane was the fingerprint of the years passed, given to the glass and taken on in silent acceptance. I rubbed the glass carefully with my hand so as not to cut myself on the cracks that looked like the outline of a map. I peered out at the overgrown shrubbery which once used to be the beautiful landscaped garden. I smiled to myself, with some hard graft and the enlisting of a few local gardeners, it could be returned to its former glory.

I turned my back to the window and looked at the room, the light caught something in the corner, near to the side of the door and made it glisten. I stepped carefully over to it and bent down for a closer inspection, trying to spread my weight evenly on the rotting floorboards. I picked it up, it was a necklace. Now, I am no antiques expert but I had previously written an article on an antiques dealer when I lived in England and in order to develop my story I had to 'shadow' him for research purposes. If truth be known, I quite enjoyed it and found it enlightening, he taught me how to sift through what initially might be considered 'junk' to find anything of any value and how to then date and price items.

CHAPTER 6

If I remember my experience correctly, it looked like a French nineteenth century lavaliere, a locket for those of us not in the antiques field. It was hung on a delicate silver chain and had a green stone in the centre of it on both sides. One side of the inset stone had been worn away a little, maybe whoever this belonged to had been given it as a special gift and wore it regularly as a reminder that they were loved and adored. I carefully brushed away the dust debris with my t-shirt, causing it to gleam once more despite it's years of abandonment. It reminded me of wet pebbles on a beach, how they shine in the sunlight, so perfect in their symphony of colours.

I gently prized open the clasp of this once precious emotional amour, it actually still had its small photographs safely housed within, albeit somewhat faded. Squinting at them, they were hard to make out but they sort of resembled Edward and Amélie Wrexham, I couldn't swear to it without a magnifying glass.

Without warning a sudden coldness entered me making me shiver, I could have sworn the locket trembled in my hands and I heard laughter, not particularly happy though, more of a rueful type. Just then Tim appeared outside the door, thank goodness as I was about to emit a loud scream. "Jaz, Are you ok? You look like you have seen a ghost,"

I smirked nervously, could that be what it was? Tim continued, "Jaz, having looked around I don't regret buying Iberville for one minute, but there is a lot more work to be done inside than I anticipated and we haven't even stepped outside yet, you think we can do it? He folded his arms and propped himself carefully against the doorway.

"Good sleuthing Mr Meyers, you are not wrong in your deductions, it's not like you to be unsure of things. I am sure it is possible, as long as you think we have the money to do it, we can conquer all. I know I was hesitant at first but I really would like us to call this home even though there is an awful lot to do." At last my confident side has come out of its shell! Tim smiled at me, "Anything's affordable for you, we can probably call in a few favours and it might be a bit tight for a while. I think we will need to renovate a bit at a time, our biggest challenge will be getting the locals to work so we will need to come up with some excellent coercion tactics." I nodded as he crouched down beside me, "What have you got there?"

I held up the locket for him to see, opening it once more so he could see the tiny pictures. "Is it worth anything?" He asked tilting his head as he tried to inspect the faded images. Then without warning the locket literally flew out of my hand and through the air, landing with a plop on the other side of the room. We looked at each other, quite spooked, perhaps there was a ghost here after, locked in another time warp, anyhow how can we be scared of the dead when the living are so volatile? I thought to myself. "Damn ghosts, out, out damn spot, a quote from lady Macbeth." Tim joked waving his hand in front of us, "I know, but actually we could have just been party to a paranormal exchange, who knows what walks these walls." I laughed.

There had been many rumours over the years since her death that Iberville was haunted by lady Amélie's ghost and that anyone who dared trespass in her grounds would suffer as a consequence. "Do you think Iberville has grown tired of the mess, the spiders and limp cobwebs and chosen to become a more fun sort of haunting, you know like the kind of house the Adams family would choose?" Tim asked "Don't say things like that, it's not funny, the last thing I need here is screaming fears of abandonments by those lost to their own pains and have no forward path or motivation." I uttered my eyes darting around the room in case there was anything or any ghostly apparition remotely visible in shadow form, there wasn't obviously!

Tim helped me up and brushed the dust off of his shorts, "We can't see them and they can't hurt us, it's the living that we need to be afraid of." He spluttered, laughing at the same time he spoke as he waggled his finger into the air adding, "If you are listening, lady Amélie or whoever you are, like it or not we are going to be living here so get used to it or preferably leave." I rolled my eyes and let out a heavy sigh before relaxing enough to laugh, Tim looked quite loopy, insane even, talking into a room of nothingness warning off any ghostly phenomenon that may be lurking, I do hope they were taking notice!

I too brushed the dust from my clothes, a bit too hard, sending a plume of debris into the air. "Are you really a hundred percent sure that we have enough money?" I asked watching Tim's amusing expression falter to a steady serious look, but one that was still sincere and full of positivity. "Yes, definitely, I have never been so sure about anything in my life, except you of course my darling." He grinned. "Let's go back to the shack for now, have something to eat and sleep on it, we can make a plan about what exactly we need to do with Iberville in the morning, I am beginning to feel quite exhausted." I nodded in agreement, he was right, time had slipped away from us and we hadn't even been home yet.

I was quite eager to be back in my shack and get some well earned rest. I have to say that can't be entirely sure I left much food in the fridge, so dinner tonight will have to be a 'make and mends' type of meal, probably something like beans on toast, in front of the telly before we retire. With all our excited plans we will end up talking and laughing amid mouthfuls of toast, spraying crumbs all over the carpet. TV dinners were never a good move.

As we left the room, I swear I felt something brush past me and form a shadow in front of the locket. When my imagination struggles to solve any problems it needs to process it and expands into areas of consciousness, hence the hallucinations, either seeing or hearing things. I learnt that from a fortune teller once, no idea if it is true or not, but definitely on this occasion something was playing tricks with me, the locket didn't move, it just lay there, the fading sun rays making it change to an amber type colour.

I took some quick photos on my phone as we made our way back downstairs, predominately to send to my folks back home, they would be impressed, if not shocked. I could hear the conversation now. My father sat in his chair with his newspaper, glancing up from it, a man of few words, not really hearing what had been said to him, so replying, "Well done Jasmine old girl," whilst my mother on the other hand, would launch into a spiel along the lines of, "What would you want with a house that big, but you know I am happy if you are happy and its what you want, I'm so very proud of you, I always knew you wanted to make a positive difference in this world. You have risen to become a voice for society that cares for all, finding the strength in your identity as a woman, blah blah."

Tims voice cut through me, "Jaz, stop daydreaming, are you coming?" by now he was standing at the huge open entrance door, I took a few more photos of the paint flaking walls and random damp patches. It would be a reminder of our achievements and what it looked like before we restored. Anyway through the camera lens, the differing sun-baked hues made Iberville's decrepitude even more beautiful.

I felt a sense of serendipity, as we closed the door behind us, albeit with some difficulty, it's rusty hinges, creaking and squeaking, echoing like the weariness of an old man. I couldn't wait to come back, tear the boards from all the windows, let the light fly inside and lift all the gloom from the rooms. I took one final photo as we stood at the bottom of the steps, it really was an impressive building and as I pinched myself once more, it really was our home.

CHAPTER 7

Thankfully, Goldie had retuned a couple of weeks earlier from her honeymoon and surpassed herself as the good friend that stands by me, no matter what. She had managed to stock me up on a few essential bits, even leaving us some freshly cooked jerk chicken, she truly was the best. So nice to arrive home and be able to slouch, we were physically and mentally exhausted from travelling and Iberville had added to that with a sort of nervous tiredness coupled with an edge of excitement. Basically we plonked our suitcases in the bedroom, ate and drank amid some lively chatter before showering and climbing into bed only to fall asleep instantly in each others arms, letting our dreamworlds take hold.

The following morning we awoke to the sun blazing through the half open curtains, its golden petal shaped rays stretching outwards onto the bedroom wall morphing into changing mosaic pictures. Tim bumbled out of bed and pulled back the fabric a bit wider in order to dictate what the day might bring, weather wise. He stretched and yawned before standing to one side. "Today's weather will be mostly warm, the deck is slick with water and the few puddles will dissolve in the sun, there seems to be no hint of rain to come, despite the gentle breeze I predict a very good day ahead." "Don't give up your day job!" I laughed, sitting up to watch a few clouds move in the morning sky, gliding over the ocean, together yet somehow independently of each other, drifting lazily in the gentle breeze without any destination or purpose. Their gaps widening and closing as they played with each other, some sliding delicately underneath, constantly morphing into different mesmerising shapes. Tim bowed before disappearing downstairs, he was so gorgeous, Those muscles, that body told a story of a man willing and able to put in daily effort to achieve a goal. He was all mine, but that said he was no weather expert.

He arrived back in record time with a cobbled together breakfast and a sort of scroll, aged white with writing in faded black ink, forever bound upon this enchanted parchment and bound with ribbon. "What on earth?" I asked, cocking my head to one side straining for a better view and pointing. I was eager to see what it was, but at the same time wanted to tease Tim. I leant forward seductively on the bed, I didn't think initially he took the bait as he uttered, "Its Iberville's plans, thought we could take a look," but then he followed it up with, "although you look like you have some mischief making planned."

He sniggered, pushing me backwards and spreading the plans on top, tickling me at the same time. I squirmed and giggled like a child as I carefully rolled out from underneath. Tim moved them to the side as I linked my fingers into his other hand and shot him a look that was all about love, with just the right hint of mischief. I grabbed him tighter, pulling him close as he kissed me, slightly bemused, he knew there was no doubting that look, a wonderfully wicked idea and all of it needed to happen in our king sized bed. God, I needed to get a grip. I returned the kiss and pulled back, sitting forward on my knees. Well, it was a tease after all. I tried to make sense of all the plans as I sipped some decaffeinated coffee.

It all looked so confusing, it was written in a way that it would take someone with intellect and a little architectural intelligence to gain any instinctive comprehension of all the old meanings, I felt quite uneducated. I took a bite of my toast, Mmhm, in the hope that it would help me digest the plans and make some sense of it, 'food for thought' and all that, to paraphrase although I am aware thats not quite what it means.

Instead the mouthful brought me solace in the purity of it's own innocence, my toasted bread was done to perfection, a honey caramel-brown colour with just the right amount of crunch despite the butter and jam melting from the gentle warmth it still retained. Then with every mouthful of the golden toasted crumb came the softness within, this jammy toast had a very good start to the morning condensed into each sweet bite.

We both studied the plans, pointing out the various paragraphs of interest, whilst becoming acutely aware that the more we looked at the expanse of land it sat on, the more it sunk in that we had definitely taken on more than we could chew. "This is going to be our biggest challenge yet, I think our best plan of attack is to break it down into more manageable chunks, almost restoring each room in turn. We will absolutely need the help of the local skilled tradesmen, but if you are on board with it, I am up for doing as much as we can ourselves." I uttered, managing to spray a mouthful of little toasted grains over Tim, the plans and the bed in the process.

Tim listened intently whilst tactfully brushing the debris from his chest and politely moving the plans to shake off any still attached toast crumbs. He turned over a page which revealed the gardens and out buildings, before replying. "Yes, definitely Jaz," then putting on an aristocratic voice said, "ma'am, you are quite correct in your analysis, I whole heartedly concur that breaking the work down into bitesize pieces will be the best way forward. However I do think we should modernised Iberville but without removing too much of its history. What do you think about us making an income from it? I have a few favours to call in, so the workforce is hopefully not going to be an issue and there is currently enough money in the pot to start, not an abundance, but enough for us to do what we want." I listened and nodded in agreement in the correct places, giggling childishly at his poor attempt to be someone he wasn't.

Tim continued, "We should keep the main house for us but change it around slightly as you mentioned when we looked around, the land would become our income, reinstate the distillery, maybe use the gatehouse as a museum, smaller cottages as living accommodation for distillery workers?" I nodded, "Yes it all seems very feasible in theory." I said as Tim took a bite of toast before saying, " However, one of my main concerns is our own work commitments, what will happen if I am called away on a mission, or you need to travel with the paper?" I nodded again, "Completely agree, but we can cross that bridge when we come to it, I am sure we will be able to work something out and I think living from the income Iberville could generate is a great idea, it will also be good for the Island as it will create a few job opportunities." I surprised myself, was this really me speaking with a new air of confidence, after all I was now the wife of a secret agent and about to be the 'lady of the manor,' so I would have to raise my game!

We lost all sense of time again, remaining on the bed in our PJ's, for the next few hours, planning expected outcomes, our interventions, rationalising and evaluating our ideas, writing them down and making lists so that we could put theory into practise more easily. It was so exciting, we were completely lost in the moment until the reality check happened. My mobile rang, it was Goldie. "Ah ha Yuh two a still alive den, can wi cum ova Ar a yuh a go inna wuk todeh?"

Oh no, the Alise, I had forgotten about work, I was supposed to be back in today, I was having so much fun until then. There was a momentarily pause until Goldie broke the silence, "Nuh worry Ave anedda day Pia hav eh all ship shape." I breathed a sigh of relief, even if she didn't, I had no intention of going into work today, much more important stuff to do on my agenda, but I needed to sound keen. "Are you sure, I could be there by ten if really needed?" "Nuh need," came the confirmation I needed from Goldie. "Come over, we have some news," I uttered trying to control the excitement in my voice and despite Tim shaking his head and waving his arms in the air like a lunatic.

There was a tiny nano second of silence before she shrieked down the phone,"Dat did quick wuk Mi will bi di bess auntie evah." Well, that didn't go quite to plan, why would she jump to that conclusion? "Good grief no, not that, some other news that does not involve being pregnant or leaving the Alise." "Oh, ok," was all she replied with a detectable hint of disappointment in her voice.

CHAPTER 8

Despite my initial reservations, the rumours were that Pia was doing a fantastic job, being in charge of the paper whilst Goldie and I had been away. She had apparently run it with absolute precision and every time I phoned her to check in, she always told me to take my time, there was no need to rush back it was all under control. I think if truth be known, she was enjoying the responsibility and power bestowed upon her, which in turn would mean she was also going to take some persuading to hand back the reins and my office if I decided to stay.

The phone clicked silent, "Goldie," I said to Tim, as if he hadn't heard the conversation, he was sat next to me desperately trying to stop me asking her to come over after all. "Yes, got that, there is no mistaking Goldie's dulcet tones" he smirked, "Is Leroy coming over with her?" He asked, "Mmmh not sure, suppose so, we'd best get dressed." Tim grinned again "plenty of time yet" he said pushing me backwards onto the bed again, I toppled over my head hitting the pillow with a soft bounce. Our PJ's suddenly became a hinderance, but that problem was solved in record time, thats covet ops training for you, quick thinking and always ready for action!

Wherever his fingers touched me, they were electric, my skin tingled in a frenzy of static as his hands continued to roam over my body. I developed a transitory paralysis, my mind a complete blur, unable to process the pleasure as fast as his head moved round to my left ear whispering what I was about to experience next. I squealed, my body now completely off pause-mode as I managed to regain some control, both of us moving together in an intoxicated dance of limbs, not making the exact same moves twice. This wasn't exactly getting dressed, but who cares as from there on in it was all about passion, intensity, intoxication. It was our release, escape. We both moaned and fell back onto the bed panting, our bodies still hot and tingling. I used to be afraid that everything would change when we married, but if anything it's made our bond and sex life so much deeper, much more sensual.

Our passionate encounter was short lived and instead turned in to operation scramble as Goldie's dulcet tones echoed through the kitchen window, which I had left slightly ajar, "Cooee Mi attracting unnu attention eena English. Aren't yuh up yet? Tap a mek out an cum an open di door." We shot a glanced with raised eyebrows at each other, "God, she is just indescribable, isn't she?" I said sighing, Tim laughed, "yep, no flies on her, looks like we will have to resume play later" he said, slapping my bottom as I rolled off of the bed and smiled as he threw on my dressing gown. I watched him as he headed out the door, it didn't seem to matter what he put on, his muscular physique just made him look so powerful, and the little fish motifs almost suited him!

I was not too far behind him, throwing my PJ's back on for convenience, I did laugh though, what would he think when he realised that it was my robe he was wearing? Anyhow we arrived clothed in some form or another, if not somewhat dishevelled just in the nick of time, as Goldie had almost climbed through the kitchen window and was surveying the scene as we arrived. "Where's Leroy?" I asked "Already in," came his reply from behind me, I jumped about ten feet in the air, "you really need to make this place more secure." He said waving my keys at me and nodding towards Tim as they both erupted into laughter. "And you missy, couldn't use the door because?" I asked grinning at Goldie, "Practising fi mi spy tactics, any coffee?" She replied, "I'm sure I can muster some more up," I replied putting the kettle on and emptying the cafetière ready for refilling.

Leroy plonked himself down at the kitchen table and patted his lap, Goldie obliged like an obedient puppy. "What are you wearing man, is that even allowed?" Leroy asked Tim looking him up and down, Tim blushed realising his apparel as Goldie announced, "Wi need tuh tell each odda all di details ah fi wi honeymoons." She said beaming, "Er no you don't, that's old news you were both on the phone to each other almost every day, what else is there to tell?" Leroy commented, admittedly he was right, our conversations were a daily occurrence. She kissed him,"Ok, yuh sexy beast, keep unnu wig pan, Waah unnu news Jaz?" I looked at Tim, who was sucking in his cheeks and trying desperately not to laugh at her doughy eyed puppy dog antics, almost as if I needed permission to speak, "Go on then, I know you are dying to, spill the beans" he gestured.

I took a deep breath before excitedly blurting out, "Tim has bought Iberville, we are going to make it our home, we will renovate it and live off of the income the land generates as a business, restore the distillery, etc." That was a long sentence, even for me, "and breathe," Tim said folding his arms around my waist.

On the contrary, neither of them looked particularly shocked, Leroy stood up, shook Tim's hand and kissed me on the cheek. "My god man, you do move in mysterious ways and without any time to loose, congratulations." Goldie on the other hand jumped in the air screaming loudly, with a kind of high pitched noise that shrilled right through our ears ready to burst any unsuspecting eardrums, it was heartfelt though and that's all that really mattered. "Whoopee, dat a fantastic news, how exciting! Missa an Mrs Meyers fram Iberville. Can wi hab di shack Mi ave eva deh waah tuh liv rite pan di beach Wah duh yuh tink baby love?"

Leroy stood silent for a moment, trying to take it all in but mostly deaf, in shock or both, much the same as Tim and I.

I did love Goldie's directness, but she never ceases to catch me off guard, having said that, she did have a point, it was a great solution. They had started married life in her rented accommodation, whilst they found somewhere to settle and we needed to move out and into Iberville to get the ball rolling so to speak, I know its a dreadful choice of words!

I glanced at Tim as I poured the coffee, "Don't look at me for the answers, sweetheart, its your place, what would you like to do with it? You can either sell it to Goldie and Leroy who will lovingly destroy it and make it their own, or let it go to a complete stranger who will do the same, but you will never see inside it again, if Goldie and Leroy have it, it will stay in the family so to speak, the decision is yours alone to make." He was right and do you know what? I made my decision in that instant. "Yes, Goldie, I would love for you and Leroy to buy my house and live in it happy ever after." She squealed again, not as high pitched this time, but still began dancing around again like a demented octopus, chanting "Wi will liv inna shack, Wi will liv inna shack.

Leroy tried to calm her, but failed miserably, it was like trying to tell a fire not to burn. Her eyes were alight and everything was tickling her as funny, for any single idea she has coming from her mouth right now, there are going to be several more queuing up in her mind. "Jaz Mi luv yuh, thank you suh much. Mi will luv dis place as yuh habaz." "We need to sort out the logistics babe, don't get too carried away just yet. Jaz, are you sure?" Leroy uttered, managing to grab hold of Goldie as she danced past him for the fourth time.

He gained back control, securing her in his arms and pulling her back onto his lap once more, trying to keep a tight grip as she squirmed. "It would be an honour." I replied, feeling like despite only halfway through the day, it was going to be up there with the best days of my life so far. I just needed the strength to make one more decision. What to do about my job at the Alise!

CHAPTER 9

Tim and Leroy walked through to the lounge with their coffee to discuss, logistics, plans, missions, general catch up etc, I grabbed Goldie by the arm, "Sit down I need to talk to you, this is serious." Goldie groaned and slumped at the kitchen table, her demeanour changed in an instant, brows creased and face tense, but there was still her feel of unwavering love.

Talking to Goldie was different from Tim in more ways than one, she's more like me than anyone else I know, she thinks inside similar walls to me but she is also able to jump right out of the ideas box and imagine dilemmas in a totally different way. That's the point of talking to her, to get what's in my head out there, to start new lines of thought and hope they ripple out into our collective "pond." I want to have a conversation where I feel invigorated afterwards instead of disturbed by the lack of mental flexibility people have not including Tim in that of course. " Wah Gwaan?" She asked, "I have a real dilemma and for the life of me, can't decide what my best option is." "Wid Tim?" "No, no, that's all perfect. Its just that I don't want to head the Alise anymore, I have been churning it around in my mind for a while now, we spoke briefly about it before we went to Anegada, remember?" "Mi duh Wah will yuh duh instead, eff yuh didn't guh bac? Duh yuh ave ah plan? Yuh need frackles." "Yes, I know, I need money and no I don't have any plans, but I know that I am not going to be happy there in the long term. I want something exciting and different in my life." "A nuh a move inna Iberville exciting enuff fi you? She replied looking bewildered. "Yes, but maybe this is the push I need to get out, Iberville will keep me busy and Tim has said that he can and is willing to support the both of us, not that I really want that, I still want my independence you understand." She nodded, " What do you think, if I go would you like to interview for the editors job with Pia?" She shook her head, quite violently before coming out with a her wacky idea. "Christ nuh, Eff yuh guh mi guh. Mi kno crazy idea, wi cud becum private investigators. Mi can jus seet now, Jewel and the Crown private investigators." Oh, how I laughed, as if there were ripples in a still pond after a stone had been thrown in. That laughter became infectious and caused the two of us to fall about tittering until the great waves of hilarity took hold.

Leroy and Tim walked back into the room, if there was a world leader board of smirkers, they would be the champions. "Forgive us for listening in on your conversation, but we need to burst your bubble, you can't actually do that." "What do you mean?" Goldie asked, her smile disappearing and a serious expression taking over, trying to appease and pretend there were no swirls of negative energy being inflicted. Leroy sighed heavily, was this really a conversation he wanted to get into with Goldie, he didn't usually win. "Because babes, you have no formal training, no offices, no clients, you could get yourselves hurt or worse killed if you don't know what you are doing. It's not something you can do on a whim and besides the name is absolutely awful." "He's right." Tim piped up siding with him, sobering words indeed, a response based in both logic and empathy rather than the jangle of our imaginative minds. "About which bit?" I asked, "All of it, I want my wife alive." Tim said kissing me on the forehead. "We can get training, Wi nuh waah tuh wuk fah di paper nuh muh." Goldie replied, once she has a firm grip on an idea, nothing is going to stop her bulldozing through even though, as usual her plan was not thought through. It was an idea that was a fantasy but could if planned properly, potentially could be worth pursuing, food for thought, there goes that cliche again, although we would definitely have to change the name.

Our conversation turned into silly banter, it was bonding, it was friendship at its best and my unsolved dilemma soon became pushed to the back of our minds. Tim looked at his watch, "Jaz, I have an idea, let's find something to wear, Leroy, Goldie can you put a snack together, I think we will luncheon at our new home Iberville today." Gosh that did sound weird and sort of lovely amongst all the dust! "Mi nuh hab fi mi bess clothes pan," Goldie remarked looking quite serious, "I wouldn't worry, whatever you wear, you will come out looking like you have been win a snow storm from all the dust, it is terrible." I replied grinning, Tim just raised his eyebrows at Leroy.

We all obeyed our instructions and set about the tasks at hand, I even went the extra mile and managed to put some washing in the machine that we had taken out of our suitcases whilst looking for something clean to put on. We dressed hastily, well I say that, but it wasn't that quick. In the end I changed tactics and gave up trying to find garments that complimented each other, instead I just threw on the nearest clean items. My mother always said, "When your clothes match your playful soul you will always feel properly dressed." I never understood what she was on about but guess this was my option today.

I managed to find a rather creased skater dress that followed my form yet gave a nice flow in the skirt, it sat a little above my knee when walking and standing, rising a few inches higher when I sat. Personally it's a comfortable degree of sexy, but I always seem to feel that it needs to be a longer length. Tim looked at me, "Come here darling, you look super sexy," he grinned pulling me into his strong arms, "are you really serious about leaving the Alise?" "I think so," came my answer, "I have not been happy there for a while, I told you a while ago that it was now all about greed and very few morals, that's not what I stand for or what I want for the Alise. I want a something different, something exciting but I don't have the courage or patience to take the next step and the trouble is, I don't have another career pathway in mind. The last thing I want is to end up with no money to help us with our plans or to make myself look stupid."

"Who would run the paper, Pia?" "Yes, probably or Goldie, although she says no, either of them are more than capable."

Tim brushed his fingers against my cheek, "You know, being brave isn't the same thing as being stupid. It pays to weigh up all the pros and cons of your actions versus your inaction, we can make a list together if you like later on. I can think of many instances that I have found myself in, where the brave choice was to stay, but, when the situation is intractable, it takes courage to remove yourself from the equation. If its truly what you want, take that step forwards and then, as if by magic, you will find the confidence, your own voice to do whatever you want. You need to do what is right for you, even if it feels like the hardest and unsafe thing to do. You're made of the right stuff, I believe in you, so you should believe in yourself." I smiled and nodded before kissing him on the lips, he was so supportive, he didn't give me the answer or try to belittle the intensity of my feelings, just a gentle nudge towards my ultimate decision.

I guess being that one step removed he can see me more clearly as a person with needs rather than a problem-creating dependancy. He returned the kiss seductively as we gazed into each others eyes, "Jaz, you know over a lifetime your decisions define who you are, already you are an accomplished person who has their own respect and love. I will support and help you one hundred percent whatever decision you make. We will talk more later, I will always listen and offer up sound advice, but not make the decisions for you." He was so fabulous, the era of valour has been reborn, he has this sense of gallantry defined by his chivalrous code, raising me up and making me feel like an equal. In fact, I can go as far as saying that in that moment, my decision was made, I will grow my feathered wings and take flight, I have the confidence and energy to take whatever direction I want to take in my new life.

We rejoined Goldie and Leroy, who were supposed to be making lunch to take with us, however they had thrown caution to the wind and were actually making out on the kitchen table, yuk, they could keep this item of furniture when they bought the house that was for sure. Thankfully some of the food had been relegated to the surrounding worktops.

It didn't take long for Goldie to become aware we were watching, she pushed Leroy off of her, "Yuh rude bwoy Wi ave squashed do lunch," she winked at him as she helped him off the table and removed some strands of lettuce and a slice of tomato from his hair.

I have to say I stopped being embarrassed by her antics a long time ago, I have learnt to adapt and overcome, another conquered goal to add to my growing list of achievements. Goldie picked up the thick cut slices of bread that they had managed to stuff with generous fillings of salad and what ever else they found in the fridge."Yuh need tuh gun shopping," She stated, "Yes, you might want to do that, everything and anything is in these sandwiches," Leroy uttered squashing the sandwiches with the palm of his hand as he tried to get the clingfilm to wrap around them, "not sure the chocolate spread and salad go well together," he winked.

From the corner of my eye I saw Tim screw up his face in agreement, "I think we best call in to Agwe's mini mart on the way, last thing we need is food poisoning" he uttered looking disgusted at the thought of having to eat Goldie's concoction. "Well, at least dem contain unnu five ah day.' Goldie retaliated. I too felt an instant relief from Tim's suggestion, it was definitely the better option looking at the squashed sandwiches that really needed to be given a decent burial in the bin!

Tim drove us all to Iberville, via the mini mart, where we stocked up on everything we needed for a much more inspiring tasty lunch. Goldie gave us earache as she chattered almost non stop about her plans for the shack, she was also so excited about seeing Iberville for real. She had only seen it in photos, she only became aware of it and its history when she supported me through the most difficult time in my life five years ago. I wonder what she will make of it now?

It wasn't too long after leaving the mini mart before we turned the corner to the hill and arrived at Iberville. We climbed out of the car and all stood for a minute, each of us with our own quiet contemplation before Goldie gasped, "Eh it's huge and very impressive." She was right, looking at it now, it's stonework carried the memory of its creation many, many years ago, handed down through Lady Amélie Wrexhams family line.

Suddenly, Goldie screeched and pointed at the window, "Can you see that?" We all looked up at one of the boarded windows, "See what? Can't see a thing." Leroy commented, Tim nodding in agreement. I on the other hand was as dumbstruck and unnerved as Goldie, by a ball of light that had appeared in front of the dark window. I blinked again, unsure as the light seemed to float and expand before our very eyes before morphing into a glowing person in a white dress. I gasped in shock, my heart pounding so hard in my chest that I thought it was going to explode. I tore my gaze away from the window, looking at Tim. "I thought you said Iberville was abandoned." Tim nodded, "You know it is why?" I whispered into his ear with a degree of fear. "There is a lady standing in the window staring at us!"

Something in the tone of my voice penetrated his head, he

took my hand and held it tightly as he stared ahead, "You see her?" Goldie and I whispered, pointing at the apparition before us. Tim and Leroy began to laugh, "Sure, it's a killer nun or worst still the ghost of the Wrexham woman come to warn us off!" Leroy joked. "Its not funny, there is definitely a woman standing in the window," I uttered raising my voice and sounded slightly irked. "Jaz, don't be so ridiculous there is nothing there, look around you, Iberville is empty came Tim's reply"

Tim was right, only the surrounding nature had managed to embrace Iberville for the last few years, the flora flowing within it as much as around it, but despite its history, for me, I felt a weird sense of belonging. Goldie and I looked again but whatever sightings we had claimed to see had now disappeared. Goldie had left us standing and had started to make her way up the stone steps to the entrance. "Eh huge Jaz, nothing like I imagined," she shouted, the image we had seen instantly forgotten about. "Be careful, watch your footing, some of the steps are loose and in need of some serious repair." Tim shouted back. She waved her arms in the air, beckoning us to follow.

CHAPTER 10

As we stood in front of those grand doors, I removed the key from my pocked unlocked the door and with some force pushed it open once more. Despite those creaks, the door seemed even more of a portal to something new, a good thing to enjoy, our challenge to make better. Iberville seemed to have become more aware of itself this time, not protesting as much at our being there.

You could still sense the pain and unhappiness echoing within the walls, but there was now an aura of wanting to break free and release itself to be reborn again. Iberville just simply needed to flow and breathe some new life. We walked towards the bottom of the huge staircase, "Some work needed here that's for sure, you can't do this alone surely?" Leroy said touching the stair rail and then removing his hand, attempting to dislodge some of the stickiness from the palm of his hand and looking upwards at the designs of fruit and flowers carved into the moulding Goldie rubbed her eyes, the dusty air giving off a cloying scent that made our eyes itch before she sneezed.

There is something so very cartoon character about sneezing, its loud and suddenness with a great proclamation to all in hearing range. As I started to answer Leroy's question, Tim touched my arm, as if to say allow me. "Yep, there sure is, but we have a plan don't we Jaz?" I nodded confidently, smiling, a growing happiness erupting from deep inside of me, much as a spring flower opening. It lit up my eyes as I enjoyed the feeling and let it spread into every part of me. I can't explain how or why but everything just felt right, I felt so vibrant and free.

Leroy and Tim disappeared off to look in the orangery and the land outside, blue prints tucked firmly under Tim's arm. He had an idea that the orangery could possibly become an indoor pool, how ostentatious could you get! As they left us, Tim began explaining to Leroy about turning the outside into a local business, bringing the plantation, mill distillery and out buildings into the modern twenty-first century. I on the other hand continued to show Goldie around inside whilst our conversation was just excited babble really. "Jaz, Mi still cyaan believe yuh a gwine actually liv yah after all that has happened here in this place," she was right, it was hard to envisage, "You know, at first, your right, I couldn't even comprehend the idea of living here, but having thought about it, I really want this, this is my chance to put the past behind me for good, renovate Iberville with our modern day designs, but keep some of its history." I paused for breath, then turning to face her I took both of her hands and held onto them tightly, "I am so excited that you and Leroy are going to be living at the shack, I know it will be in the best hands and it is a great start for both of us, we will be able see each other everyday, even when I leave the Alise." "So you are going to leave then?" Goldie asked, "Yes, it is the right thing to do isn't it?" I could hear myself almost needing her approval. She smiled.

Goldie continued to explore the downstairs, with me close at her heels pointing out areas of interest and giving brief descriptions of what we were thinking of doing. She made her way into what used to be the drawing room and looked around stepping over the abandoned debris that was strewn everywhere you trod. I could tell she was definitely impressed although very daunted by the grand scale of everything, "It's amazing, such a lot of work though. Will yuh bi all yah so, a eh definitely wah yuh want?" She asked, looking at me concerned at what Tim and I were about to take on. I do wish she would decide to speak either English or Jamaican and not both in the same sentence, it was very confusing. "Goldie, it will be fine, we will just renovate it in bite size pieces, it is exactly what we both want," she smiled half heartedly, she obviously would need a bit more convincing.

Just as I finished my sentence, we both looked at one another, she was aware of it too, an unusual smell of perfume began to waft through the air followed by a distinct burning smell like cigarette smoke. It was odd, one minute it was just a dank, rusty metallic aroma of wet wood and stone, the next this sweet smell of flowers and meadows. The door to the room creaked and I swear it moved a bit, along with the window rattling, as if the wind was rustling paper through a broken gap, anyone would think this house is possessed!

Goldie and I stood rooted to the spot, silent, as footsteps echoed on the stairs, followed by a sort of wailing laughter. Suddenly a dusty glass vase fell off of the mantlepiece and smashed to the floor, we both jumped. We were scared witless, I felt like I was retreating inside myself, I felt vulnerable. Goldie broke the silence, "There are ghosts here for sure, damn things, blustering around screaming. We should usher them out." I nodded tentatively as I felt a phantom hand on my shoulder and a puff of breath on the back of my neck. "Did you feel that?" I managed to say to Goldie, she shook her head, just as I felt the sensation of being grabbed on the arm and pinched. I jumped again, "get off me," I shouted brushed myself, I shivered, a feeling of light-headedness and nausea followed as the hair rose on my arms.

I walked over to Goldie who was now by the window rubbing the glass with the sleeve of her jacket, trying to peer through and see the land outside. It wasn't that successful, the glass was quite opaque from lack of care and a thick layer of dirt had managed to adhere itself to it, only willing to let a few sparse diamonds of sunlight flow through. She wiped her hands on her trousers, a filthy stripe now appeared, but she didn't seem bothered as she uttered. "If it's what you want and you can be at peace with your decision then I am happy too, you will be missed at the Alise, you are an excellent role model, but I will come with you too, we can do something together, we are almost joined at the hip after all." Gosh she had been weighing this up in her head all the time, a welcome distraction probably from our paranormal activity around here. She truly was my best friend, my life long stability when my world goes nuts and I am glad she is with me.

When I think about it, together we have navigated, grown and followed all of our passions, we have changed so much and we are both better people for it. We have this easy going camaraderie that ignites a forever friendship, our pilot light will never go out but instead always remain bright and strong no matter what is thrown at us in life. Goldie is my rock and I hers, helping both of us come to terms with past events that happened here at Iberville. Goldie has always listened, empathised and supported me, shown me how to become strong again and learn not to give up, but instead how to process and overcome my troubles.

I stood staring out of the window, the colourful rays of the sun, the shabbiness and shadows of this spooky house are artwork ready to play and continue to scare. It was all in my mind, there were no ghosts, just Goldie, to keep my sanity at this moment in time. She was amazing, if I had to describe her in a sentence I would say, she was a feminine mosaic of chaos born full of happiness.

Past memories of Iberville flashed through my mind again, I trembled, goosebumps spreading themselves over my arms, in a shiver that was a moment of truth, a past story of emotions that no mask could ever hide. "A yuh ok hun?" Goldie's voice cut into the beginning of my nightmare and brought me back to reality quickly. "Yes, just thinking about Winston and Candice again," I replied, "well nuh, Yuh cyaan change di paas Buh yuh can change di fucha." She said firmly.

Why is she always right, just like my mother, of course, everything happens for a reason, although it can't always be seen at the time. "About the Alise?" She asked as we wandered into yet another room with so much work to be done. "Mmhm, I'm listening, do you want the editor job? I can swing it your way." "Nuh tanks Mi mean wah mi seh Off yuh guh mi guh. Besides Leroy an mi waan tuh extend di shack eff dat ok? Shall we really try and turn our hands to detective work? mi tink wi wud bi gud at ih." I tried not to show too much negativity, but she was completely fixated on becoming a Private Investigator and if I'm honest it was one of those girlhood dreams for me too. However I was not about to do it on a whim, it would have to be properly researched, thought through and planned out properly after all it would be my source of income, if I was to continue down the independent but married route. "Mia totally serious, my uncle can help us, he is the Commissioner remember?" Oh yes, of course, I had forgotten about her uncle in the Police Federation with all his connections.

A soft sense of happiness had made itself at home on her face, transmitting its way to me, a glow of warmth bubbled inside, her happiness was contagious. "Are you completely sure about this, you don't have to give up your job at the Alise because of me. I have to admit if I didn't become a journalist I would have tried to join the police. Do you think we could really make this PI business work as a lucrative income for us on the Island?" I asked her. She was just about to reply when Leroy and Tim silently reappeared behind us giving us a bit of a fright. "Do what?" Leroy asked "Become Private Investigators." I replied turning to face them. Leroy couldn't contain himself and collapsed in hysterics, "Are you both still on that tact, can you honestly see yourselves as investigators? Ladies, this is one harebrained idea that needs knocking on the head right now." Tim just smirked, changing the subject he pretentiously remarked, " Let's go and eat in the orangery." Leroy raised his eyebrows as we all followed Tim, we were like four ducks in a row.

 I removed some drapes from the furniture and tried to brush away some of the dust at the same time, but all I did was make things so much worse, plumes of fine sand like particles erupted into the air causing a flurry of coughs and a few rabbit quality sneezes. For the foreseable future no matter what we did there was going to be this huge vortex of dust following us. Goldie said it was the pixies that live here, throwing their flour into the air, but unlike confetti or glitter it was so light gravity had no way to make it fall, so it would swirl in the air above like a glorious cloud changing colours with the sun-rays reflecting on it. I don't care what ever form this dust took on, all I know is that every time it is released into the air, we all end up choking.

Goldie cautiously sat on a chair, "Jaz an mi waah tuh mek dat transition, afta all Ih a betta fah wi tuh staat all di training an mek di fucha betta. Mi hab did call fi mi uncle he tink eh ah criss idea." She said kissing Leroy on the lips trying to silence him before he had a chance to launch into a less than helpful sermon. "I'm just teasing you, babes, if it's really what you both want and you both seriously think you can make a career from it, then do it. I am sure I speak for Tim as well when I say we will support you both with this crazy idea, but I want you to promise us that you will do your research first, it's not an easy profession to take on and it will always involve an element of risk, dangerous situations or liaisons. However if you think you both can handle it, you only live once, although I suspect, knowing you two sex pots, you will resemble cats." Leroy replied. Blah blah sermon over, Goldie asked "What do you mean we are like cats, my hunky monkey?" "We have nine lives, like a cat, that's how the saying goes!" I interjected before either of them could make any more lewd comments, "What's a saying?" she replied. "A sentence that people often say that gives advice or information about an experience, a cat has nine lives is the actual saying, which means they often survive dangerous incidents." I answered "Oh," she replied still looking puzzled, "we will keep managing to get out of difficult or dangerous situations without being hurt or harmed." I concluded. She laughed as Tim stuck his forth pennyworth in and uttered, "Unless you are a political cat of course, they seem to have far more than nine lives." Well, that did finish us off with a guffaw of laughter echoing around the orangery.

Suddenly I darted to one side, "What was that?" I asked, touching my arm, I was convinced something had just brushed past me and poked me, "Just that duppy," Goldie smirked, "that's not at all funny," I replied looking around the room for any concrete evidence of her deduction. "A what?" Tim and Leroy asked at the same time in a high pitched questioning voice whilst sniggering childishly at the word. We had all gotten used to Goldie's language over time but despite being able to converse in perfect English on newspaper interviews, she always reverted to talking in her own heritage dialect 'Patois' with us. "It means a ghost." I replied as we all fell about with hysterical laughter once more amid the mushroom cloud of dust that was now circling lower around us.

Amid mouthfuls of lunch we all plotted planned and laughed, before leaving Iberville and going back to our respective homes. Goldie and I agreed to set aside some researching time at work tomorrow and Tim and Leroy would contact their handlers to see what their next missions were, if any. We could then all start to finalise details and put our best laid plans into practise, if only it was going to be that straight forward!

CHAPTER 11

The following morning I headed for work at the Alise with as much positivity as I could muster, albeit with some trepidation. It was my first day back at the paper in what seemed ages. The Alise had been left in the hands of the very accomplished Pia who despite my initial reservations had done an outstanding job in my absence.

I was quite anxious, I know that sounds silly, it felt like I was starting school again, butterflies in my stomach and that gnawing aching nausea feeling as nervous emotions and anxiety continue to loom. I kept telling myself that all will be okay, but I can't quite seem to persuade my inner brain to get rid of its electrical storm that, quite honestly, is becoming irritatingly painful, a type of throbbing headache mixed with a frozen panic that has nowhere else to go. Although I probably appeared calm and collected on the outside, inside I continued to scream, "Help me, help me."

I needn't have worried as walking into the office everyone clapped, cheered and seemed genuinely pleased to see me back. Colby even thrust some flowers at me which I duly accepted and thanked everyone. I don't know why I had got myself in such a state and as I relaxed it felt like I had never been away, the same old, same old.

Pia appeared at the doorway of my office to greet me and welcomed me in which felt a little weird, normally I was the one doing that. She cleared away the paperwork she was working on and stacked it in a neat pile on the desk before moving like a clockwork soldier to the other side, ushering me to sit in my chair and instantly handing me back my editor reins.

I sat down in my chair, it felt ok, but not right, those feelings of wanting to leave still played on my mind, it was the right time to go, I felt sure. Coffee was brought in courtesy of Goldie, in truth I knew it wouldn't be long before she appeared and took up her usual stance, resting against my desk. She stared at Pia with one of her disapproving looks making her squirm and feel slightly awkward. "Thanks Goldie, that will be all for now, I need to catch up with Pia." I commented, she nodded and without further ado removed herself from my office.

The air felt so brittle it could snap, Pia let out a slow controlled breath in an attempt to loosen her body, she gave her shoulders a wiggle and lolled her head in a circle. Her eyes moved with the alertness that comes from heavy stress and her hands remained clenched by subconscious demand. It was a decent enough effort to fool the casual observer, but for the onlooker with a keen eye she was a walking advert for tension.

I poured the coffee in an attempt to try and calm her, she smiled nervously before speaking, "Did you have a good time travelling the Islands?" She asked. "Yes, brilliant, it was great fun, thank you, we did and saw a lot, I can show you some photos on my phone later if you would like?" She nodded, "Yes please I would like that." I smiled, "So what's been happening here? Anything exciting?" Pia took a sip of her coffee and munched on one of Goldie's lime biscuits, made fresh this morning, as she brought me up to speed with everything.

There were a few local break in's that had been reported, the usual drug trafficking patrols and a new ferry service was about to be brought into operation to aid the flow of food around certain areas of the Caribbean. However, the main article that the Alise was giving full exposure to focused on the Prime Minister of the Federation of St Kitts and Nevis. He had held a marathon of one-on-one consultations that formed part of the celebrations to mark the 28th anniversary of his election as a Parliamentarian. He had been in power since 1993 and wanted to commemorate his legacy under the theme 'Touching Hearts and Transforming Communities'.

Apparently, there was an extraordinarily high turnout of locals, so much so that the Prime Minister was not able to see everyone, instead he promised that his Constituency Secretariat would contact all those he was unable to see and answer any questions. The Alise took the point of view that it was a good exercise in 'open' democracy. There was some excellent coverage and incisive reporting as a result of which our viewing statistics had rocketed, well, done Pia!

Feeling quite proud of her achievements, Pia seemed to relax a bit and followed it up by saying, "When any form of breaking news is tethered to truth and reason and is capable of seeing events from many perspectives, it always gets good results. Presenting ungrounded hearsay as truth causes a form of psychological damage to all parties." She was quite passionate about the media being held to high standards whilst having the freedom to speak about whatever we wanted, but only as long as we were able to back it up with facts, logic and reasoning.

Listening intently, she reminded me of a younger version of myself when I first started in the business, I had a passion for Journalism then, instead of the disdain I had for it now. These days I seemed to take a more cynical stance, ideals in every aspect of public life are being bent, warped to the dominant obsession of the moving times, in other words, how to make the most money or how to be the most popular with the electorate. The media was no more than pretty wrapping for all, one that was honed in to get the "consumers" in the right mood to purchase and believe all the messages it wrote. The media of the twenty-first century meant controlling all articles, sometimes it employed simple violence and intimidation techniques if it had to. People are easy to control with fear and greed, and that is true right up to the very top. Anyone who disagrees and wants to make some unprecedented statement, can easily be met with an "accident" or in some cases a hushed up assassination.

I had tried to keep abreast of everything that the Alise had reported on whilst I had been away, but I had definitely missed a few good stories, well I can't be looking at work all the time, I do have a life! "You have done an amazing job Pia, have you enjoyed it?" I asked gaining eye contact, she nodded and slightly subdued answered, "Yes, thoroughly, I really enjoy working for the Alise and for you Jaz. If I am honest I feel a bit sad to loose the responsibility I have had now you are back, I am one of those people who thrive as a leader. Oops, sorry, that sounds rude, please don't take that the wrong way." I smiled then laughed, trying to put her at ease. "Well, Pia, there may be an option here, which means you don't loose the responsibility or leadership," she stared at me, confusion written across her face, "what do you mean?" I could tell she was apprehensive wanting to know but not wanting to know what I meant, if you catch my drift.

It's a natural emotion when you don't know what's coming next. I replied with a question rather than responding to her, poor Pia, she must have felt like she was having a game of strained verbal tennis, words bouncing back and forth but getting nowhere. "Where do you see yourself in the next two years? I asked her, she nervously took another sip of coffee then swallowed hard, as if the lime biscuit had become a piece of cardboard and no amount of chewing made it possible to swallow, her mouth acting as if it was dryer than a sandbox in summer. She tried to avert my gaze as she replied, "Umm, well, if I ever got the chance, possibly doing your job, sorry, sorry Jaz, you did ask." She replied blushing as her embarrassment announced itself. I smiled again, well at least there was an honesty in her blush, she was true to her nature and herself.

I walked round to the other side of my desk and precariously perched myself in front of her, just as the office door opened and Goldie reappeared. "Hab yuh did tell har yet?" She uttered. Agh, Goldie could be so annoying at times, despite my love for her, "Just about to, would you mind giving us a few more minutes." I asked trying to give Goldie one of my sterner looks but remain calm and in control of the situation rather than being reactive. Luckily she got the hint and disappeared, winking at me as she went.

Pia looked even more confused, her shoulders had become drawn to gravity and her eyes looked sad as if she had built some new walls around her so as not to get hurt. "I know what you are going to say," she uttered, "really, tell me," I replied. She paused and heaved a deep breath. "Well, last one in and all that, you have enjoyed working with me, I am good at my job but you need to let me go, you could find me a job with all the responsibility and leadership somewhere else for me if I want to continue in a managerial role."

I stared at her for a moment before speaking. How on earth had I managed to let her think this. "Stick with me on this Pia, clarity comes with patience and time, you couldn't be further from truth if you tried. Pia, you have done a fantastic job, it can't have been easy as the new kid on the block, stepping into my shoes and running the show whilst I have been away. Now that really does show true courage, determination and good leadership skills. You've got what it takes to lead this lot and you are a realist too, you listen to logic, reason and to science, but one thing I must stress is, you need to make sure you listen to your own needs as well." Pia nodded. "Remember a leader needs to keep themselves in good condition if they are to take their workforce into battle, leading is a marathon, not a sprint."

Pia smiled nervously, listening intently as she fidgeted awkwardly in her chair, I couldn't keep her in suspense any longer. "How would you like to continue as editor for the Alise?" There was an initial silence as her eyes met mine, not quite understanding or believing what I had just asked her. She unclenched her white hands letting the blood flow through them once more, "W..what…t do you mean? I d..d… don't understand," She stammered. "Pia, I an asking you if you want to continue as the boss here at the Alise?"

By now Pia had the face of a china doll, she had taken on a pale look, as if she'd been painted with white-wash, even her lips were barely there. Quickly I managed to get her to sip her coffee and stuff another lime biscuit in her mouth before she had chance to clock out on me, I am not good with people fainting. Whilst she regained some composure I continued to whittle on, "I want a fresh start you see, I am fed up with journalism and am becoming far to cynical to lead the Alise in the direction it needs to go, I want something completely different. I have been toying with the idea for a long time now, but I have now come to the decision of pursuing a different career path and I want to leave the Alise in good hands. So that means I would like you to continue as editor and take the paper forward into the twenty-first century."

As Pia regained her composure, she let herself manage a smile, "A…are you a….absolutely sure about this? I….I would truly love to accept the permanent p…position of editor, t.t..thank you so m…much for this o..opportunity." With that Pia's eyes welled up and a few rogue tears fell onto her cheeks, tears of joy experienced in a moment that will never fade, an emotional feeling of true happiness! I continued, handing Pia a tissue, "Goldie and I are to become partners as private investigators, obviously we will need to be trained in everything to do with PI work." I felt a huge weight lift off my shoulders after I had said it, then after an awkward second or two, the corner of Pia's mouth twitched into her cheek. "P…private Investigators, you and Goldie?" she uttered, trying her hardest to control her smirk. I am not sure why everyone thinks it is funny for Goldie and I to do such a job.

There was another awkward silence which thankfully was broken by the appearance of Goldie, who irritatingly must have been listening on the other side of the door. In English the uttered, "We are going to be great Private Eye's, Jewel and the Crown, if you ever need us, remember the name." Pia's shoulders began to shake as all attempts to contain her laughter failed miserably. How rude and after everything I had just said, why on earth was it so funny to everyone? The name possibly?

Luckily she managed to restore some professionalism quite quickly as she saw Goldie and I shoot an exasperated look at each other. "Would either of you consider some freelance work from the Alise?" Pia asked. "Possibly, we need to see how things go. I plan to stay for the next month to ensure a thorough handover to you, clear out my emails, wind down my bits and pieces etc and Goldie will do the same, that gives you time to promote or hire a new reporter and feel super comfortable in your new permanent role." Pia nodded before rising to her feet and shaking my hand as Goldie began to dance, jump and giggle her way around my office as if some psychotic illness had taken hold. "Don't mind her," I smirked.

The constant tapping of computer keyboards from the outer office became drowned out by Goldie's squealing, shrieking and whoops of delight. Even a dog barked outside my window in protest as she continued to make a complete buffoon of herself, no-one seemed to mind, it was just Goldie being Goldie after all.

CHAPTER 12

I drove back to my shack that evening after work, feeling a sense of calmness and contentment anchored to my being. I have faced the arduous task of letting go of the Alise reins and won, so now I feel ready to take on the rest of the world.

As I opened the door, Tim was sprawled out on the sofa, feet twitching to music only he could hear, his face passive as if he was asleep. I moved in closer and knelt down next to him, touching his skin lightly, he jumped a little as he opened his eyes. He sat up removed his headphones and kissed me, His voice tumbling out softly, "Hey, sweetheart," I put my ear to headphones to listening to the music still playing, he smiled, "Ah, Freddie Mercury, he will always be my champion, we music fans are that way, I guess. I find so much truth in lyrics, so much humanity especially when the world news around us appears as utter madness. Love is our truth and songs always say it best, managing to shine lights upon our hearts so that we can see it from many angles, rendering it in three dimensions, allowing it to beat and base society in what is real." I just grinned, O'dear, Freddie Mercury, I have found Tim's nemesis and what on earth was he talking about. Tim grinned too before asking, "How was your day?" "Good, I think! I have resigned from the Alise and asked Pia take over, I have said I will be there for the next month handing over and possibly do some freelance work after that for extra money. I really hope I have done the right thing. Goldie and I are going to pursue our crazy private detective idea! How was your day?" I whispered, leaning in for another kiss as I gazed like some love sick puppy into his beautiful gleaming eyes.

Tim pulled me close, wrapping his arms around me with a strong hug, stronger than anything I've ever known, as if holding me wasn't quite enough, he needed to feel every ounce of me pressed in to him. It was one of my favourite times, I felt so safe in our bond. "Jaz, darling, I have told you before, you know I will support you whatever you decide, we have enough money for now, so that is not a concern." I nodded as I kissed him on his warm tender lips, he responded before saying. "Renovating Iberville will take up a lot of our time, especially if I need to go away, but this is our road to an epic adventure with a degree of fog and chill, but I am so glad that both our hearts want to grab it and let our brave feet travel it, we will need our bold eyes to stay open to all the challenges that we will meet on the way." Gracious what has he been sniffing today? "Do you have any missions yet?" I asked. "No nothing concrete, there is possibly something in the pipeline, a tradition that needs examining, is all I am permitted to say for now." Tim replied winking at me. "Oh, you mean like spy talk, um, breaking the china?" I replied feeling quite proud of myself. It's a diplomatic phase I had picked up from one of Leroy's spiels. Tim laughed, "Do you even know what it means?" Not wishing him to think I was ignorant, even though I had absolutely no idea, I tossed my head back laughing "Yes of course, it is intended as a reassurance that traditions that are held as sacred, can be re-examined and changed if they are to counter to an objective of attaining inclusion and a welcoming environment for all." Phew, that was a mouthful, I even amazed myself by almost managing to remember verbatim what Leroy had said. I still had absolutely no idea what I was talking about!

Tim laughed at me again and said, "Leroy?" I nodded, following him as he made his way into the kitchen to make our supper. "You are funny, do you even have any clue as to what you have just said?" I grinned, "Honestly? No, not really!" Tim grabbed me and tickled me, "You know words can be problematic on two important levels right? I nodded, oh God what had I gotten in to? He was about to respond with a sermon way above my comprehension. "Breaking china will ping at the subconscious or conscious levels depending on cultural sensitivities. Firstly, nobody should ever want to break another nation, especially one as large as China. Our goal is always peace first, to see the real and important needs and then try to come to the together as equals, who all wish to build an equitable world together. From such times as the opium trade onwards, let's say, China has always had legitimate difficulties with the "west" that are rarely acknowledged with the seriousness they deserve." I yawned trying to show I was already bored and he was only halfway through.

Tim continued, "The second point is "China" also brings to mind Chinese people who nationally and ethnically, both at home and globally, promote an emotional indifference and potentially cruel attitude....." "Ok, ok, enough!" I shouted jokingly, putting my hands over my ears and stopping him before he could say anything more. We both giggled noisily, a cross between a snort and a drunken laugh, his speeches always made me laugh, but I rarely understood them. "Have you told your parents about the Alise yet?" He asked changing the subject. "Yes, I phoned mum this afternoon from work, she was quite shocked but also excited for us. She wants us to be happy and if we were happy, then she was happy, she couldn't wait to tell Mrs Pollock and the vicar about Iberville."

Tim smiled, "She yelled to dad that their status in the world had been raised, they were now related to nobility and they would need to get the china out!" Tim spat out a mouthful of juice he was now drinking as he snorted with another laugh. "I know," I said raising my eyebrows, "I'm not sure she was entirely convinced about the private investigator career pathway though, she sounded a little disappointed that I was giving up a lifetime job opportunity, but at the end of the day she just wants me to be sure I am at peace with my decision. She can't wait to come and stay at Iberville, she is taking dad

shopping for new tropical attire!" Tim smirked "Poor dad."he
replied raising his eyebrows once more as we sat down to
wine and a chicken curry he just happened to have made
earlier.

My mother always understood the significance of things, she
was that listening ear, who wrapped me in her love with her
soft smile and kind words. She always put the needs of others
above hers, she was so unselfish. She is my number one
supporter before Tim that is, my angel and my hero. If I
mature to be half as good as her I will be so proud of myself.
Everyone needs a mother like mine, a never depleting
repository of love and good feeling combined with a lifetime
of experience.

We finished our meal amid more talk about Iberville and
where we should plan to start first. Luckily we both sang
from the same page, suggesting that we would renovate one
room at least and then move from the shack into Iberville
and continue with the massive renovation project.

Once we had moved in, our next step would be to call in
some favours and get the distillery working again, that would
then help with some extra income along with some added
freelance work from me if we needed it, this was so exciting.
Initially I thought making the decision to leave the Alise
would have a lingering sadness, but instead it was like an
instant release, an overwhelming sense of freedom, I had so

many excited butterflies in my stomach. I wouldn't have anyone to impress, just Tim and there would be no more media schedules to adhere to. Amazing! Now I could have some time to be philosophical, notice the small changes in society and reawaken my inner idealist.

Over the next month or so, we both wore ourselves into the ground, me winding down and leaving the Alise and the Iberville renovation project getting off to a good start. We pulled the place apart, plastic coverings off the window sills, only to reveal real wood beneath, quite pretty and totally restorable, there were definitely some strong bones in places under the old wallpaper and stains, a great foundation upon which to build up our new home.

We painted a couple of good walls white and then had a rainbow paintball fight, that coupled with the polished wooden floors and neat trim, it looked great and every splotch reminded us of fun times, renovation had never been so much fun! Don't get me wrong there were a few choice swear words from all of us as tiredness set in but, we refused to let it beat us.

Slowly we did up the one room we had chosen, we stripped cleaned and decorated, it felt lighter and brighter, becoming a room that was the beginning of a welcoming home that would eventually emerge. Our limbs constantly asked us to rest, to find somewhere warm and cozy, to simply enjoy the sunshine and stay right there. Our brains felt as if they were on a treadmill and wanted us so much to press stop. Everything about us, from the muscular aches to the emotional pull toward lethargy, the fatigue was overwhelming at times, yet Iberville had no empathy for such matters, we needed to get this one room renovated.

I handed the reins of the Alise completely over to Pia and Goldie did the same to a new up and coming reporter named Brandon. He was a bit of a "know it all," but over to Pia to reign him in. Phew! Goldie and I spent less and less time at work and more and more time packing up my shack and Goldie's rental pad ready to move to our respective new homes. Leroy and Goldie started to put their plans in place to extend the shack before Tim and I had actually moved out. I didn't mind, it was nice to see the old place morphing into something new.

Every day we were all exhausted, our bodies, our brains, our tired, tired souls, could testify that we have worked at full tilt for what seems so long with very little sleep to accompany it. If you think about it, it isn't kind to run a horse into the ground so why is it kind to let us do it to ourselves?

CHAPTER 13

After all our hard work and what seemed like an eternity, the day finally arrived, thank goodness because I don't think any of us could work another day, we all packed up our wares and were ready to move.

The shack, my safe haven for so long has lost its furniture and has now become a population of boxes that fill the house as fast as it empties, they become an act of joy, of self love. I go onwards to pastures new and the home I have loved, the walls that have protected me will now protect and become a home for Goldie and Leroy.

I had neatly labelled the boxes and written "fragile" on the sides of some in bold red letters in the hope that our helpers would take great care of those specific ones. Everything precious to us was in those boxes, some sentimental things, some not so, but they all bring back such wonderful memories to Tim and I. They were all wrapped in pastel tissue paper ready to go any place we want with them.

The removal van finally arrived, well actually it was more of a monster belching truck with dented and rusted bodywork, it looked like it was time to send it to the reconditioning yard, hopefully it would last just in time to manage to transport our possessions. I had found them via a local newspaper advertisement, they sounded quite good on paper but seeing them in the flesh I was now not so sure.

Hal the driver informed us that he had fitted the truck out with 'one of those electric converters' he had found on the roadside, so now it was a lot more environmentally friendly and could go much faster! Tim laughed as he ran his hands over the dirty rusted bodywork commenting that it was quite possibly time to send it to the car crusher and turn it into a sugar cube. I think Hal and his mate Greg were quite offended by Tim's assessment of their beloved workhorse.

Their manner changed to one of slight tension and a tightness in their faces was visible as their eyes began to move more robotically, like a clock ticking in their head, perhaps that's the countdown to an exploding temper and refusal to move our stuff if there were anymore rude comments. I nudged Tim, after all things have a time and a place, I find a well placed glare can help avoid any further confrontation. I needed to be sure he would say nothing further that could be misconstrued.

Both Hal and Greg were of large build, I swear they were each two full seats on any airline and seemed to live life as if to dispel any suggestions that fat should be auto-linked to jolly. All personality traits are gender neutral, everyone is a blend of glorious hues, who each develop different desires.

Who we eventually become is a journey of discovery, our own internal experience. Not sure what happened as far as Hal and Greg were concerned, they were the most sullen and cynical people I think I had ever come across and I had met a fair few characters in my time. Nothing was sugar coated they just fired the facts to you straight, anyway they were not that expensive and despite their poor customer relations, they would soon be out of our hair, we just needed them to do the job at hand first.

The time had come, that bitter-sweet time of parting, so much nervous excitement was bouncing between us, but I felt ready to make this move. My mother often said that a house is the one thing that always stays where it is, it is the people who move to journey on to a new chapter, a fresh beginning.

A fresh start is a good thing for all of us to do but despite the excitement, it still feels weird, as if everything that has happened to this point in time is a prequel to what comes next. The chaos has within it a sprinkle of my destiny. It will bring a new perspective, an opportunity for me to learn and become stronger as an individual. So odd or not goodbye Jasmine Tormolis, hello Mrs Jasmine Meyers. I am ready for us to embark on our new story and make the best memories of our lives.

Tim and I climbed in to our respective cars, Tim in front ready to lead the truck, we waved to Goldie and Leroy, who were now stood at the front door of the shack, arm in arm, it suited them, they will be very happy there I am sure. I surveyed the brick walls that had been my cocoon, my sanctuary for so long, letting my eyes wander over their rugged clay surface, bright in colour yet with an earthen feel. I knew leaving this home was never going to be easy, but at least I can take all the emotions and memories with me and its not like I am never going to see the place again now is it?

The entourage travelled the short distance to Iberville, I kept looking in my mirror now and again, checking the truck was able to keep up with us. I was slightly embarrassed to have the old banger of a truck belching, rumbling and stinking the neighbourhood out with its fumes filling the air with polluted smoke like some chemical soup. I tried hard to ignore the black smog that followed us, making art forms in the sky, as it flowed and swirled up from the exhaust.

We are frogs in the water, right? The temperature slowly rising, the pollution levels going up each year, yet all the time we produce more waste, more smoke, more pollutants, every bit of our ecosystem in distress. We have all the advantages and ability to live on a pristine planet of rich natural beauty, but instead we continue to squander it chasing after material wealth, well, thats enough of my philosophy, I am supposed to be concentrating on driving.

We parked the cars in our drive and began to climb the steps to the huge doors armed with the plans, it felt so good. Iberville is the sanity of the hills, the ever present home waiting for its big rejuvenation to begin. I paused for a moment to let the happiness soak right through my bones, I wanted to feel like this forever. I closed my eyes to savour the moment, never releasing the grip on the seemingly inconsequential pieces of paper full of our plans and dreams, I felt so happy, so relaxed.

Then the shouting started from below, not anger but sheer exasperation riding in their tone. "You have to be kidding, you seriously want us to carry all this stuff up these steps? It's not part of our job description and my back would never survive" came the dulcet voice of Hal. "No, no, man, absolutely not. Follow the drive to the left in your truck and we will meet you, we can bring it all in through the orangery" Tim yelled back, signalling with his hand a sort of left turn. "Are we going in then Mrs Meyers?" Tim asked me, "Yes, yes, just taking it all in." I replied looking at the reflective greens of the landscape that were now glowing brighter in the strengthening light and trying to ignore the moans, groans, huffing and puffing, coupled with a few choice words from Hal and Greg below.

I opened the huge door, this time it didn't creak, it felt like a hug upon our return, breathing a sigh of relief that it could be healed. It was still an absolute mess but luckily we had found the time to clear away some of the debris when we renovated our one and only room. It happened to be our bedroom, we thought that was the best place to start, a haven to retreat to at least.

The bedroom was a creative eclectic chaos that told a story of both our talents and obsessions, a room with plants and flowers in bloom, calming pastels and soulful browns. Despite its chaotic arrangement it still invited a serene dreamy atmosphere for us to relax in.

Although we had only renovated one room, the house already felt lighter and brighter, as if it was slowly waking up. Having said that, the walls still felt cold to the touch, as if it could steal the heat from our warm fingers, not really caring if it froze the rest of us in the process. But we will give Iberville the chance to become a real home again and bid farewell to any spirits if there are that have been its spectral company for a long time.

It would still take quite a while though, the rest of the house resembled the beginnings of a building site, a place of absolute caution and where in England we would be adorned in all sorts of health and safety apparel. For the next however how long it took, we would be camping out with our unpacked boxes, only a kettle, cups and a tin of biscuits were readily unpacked to keep us going for now.

Our furniture was unloaded from the truck and put into the orangery, dropped boxes kicking up dust bunnies the size of golf balls and causing great swirls of grime in the white morning light. Hal continued to moan about his state of ill health, crick in his neck, muscles that ached and a pain in his head, blah, blah. Gregg said very little but began to wheeze, he sounded really squeaky. He reached for his inhaler and took a puff, holding it in for a count of four before slowly expelling the air, then put the cap back on and jammed it deep into his pocket, the last thing he needed was it falling out whilst he unloaded everything.

I found myself apologising, there was so much dust and dirt everywhere, floorboards, walls, curtains and windows, there was no escape from the powdered grime that had made this house its home for now. Oh well, it was going to get a lot worse before it got better but we were prepared for that.

CHAPTER 14

The morning after our first night at Iberville I wanted to wake up really slowly and relaxed, letting the day come softly into focus. Usually waking up is my transition from the world of dreams into a real day, so it is good for my soul to take a little time, pondering the messages of my dreams and feeling ready to greet the day ahead.

However, I had had a somewhat disturbed night, Tim slept through it all. I remember closing my eyes only to find them open again and thats when it all started to happen. Oh my God! The bedroom was dark and so creepy. I lay there in the silent darkness for a moment, holding my breath I was scared, I knew there was something hidden in this darkness. Suddenly, something touched my chest, I swear it was a human hand. I was going to roll onto my side, but as I adjusted my eyes to the darkness a noise from behind me made me stay perfectly still, all this creepiness was too much. Then the sound of feet hitting the floor loudly followed by someone running towards me from the other side of the room ready to take a flying leap. "Hello, who's there," I called out trembling. Tim stirred but did not wake up. Silence! The lights flickered and the curtains rippled as if from a short flurry of an incoming breeze. I shivered, it was freezing, I wriggled further under the sheets, not sure how I thought they were going to protect me, but I then must have dozed off to sleep.

I continued to dream of the paranormal realm and woke again sometime in the middle of the night after a nightmare where I was being killed by a grotesque monster. I reached out for a glass of water only to catch sight of a woman wearing a white flowing dress holding a knife in her hand grinning and threatening to strike. So, afraid of her next move, I laid very still staring and biting my lip so as not to scream, trying to rationalise the noises and sights I was hearing and imagining. Trouble was, I couldn't think of any logical explanation, except that this wasn't a dream and Iberville really was haunted.

Even if this was an hallucination it felt the same as being tormented for real, it brought back all of the emotions and trauma from my real life kidnapping ordeal. The visual demons soon disappeared without causing any harm but the noises continued as I lay awake too frightened to move. Night turned into early morning, my insomnia ignited by real fear, a kind of sleep deprivation that is painful. I did eventually fall asleep but for not very long, I would then awake as if I was breathing for the first time, as if my body was deprived of oxygen. The only way out is a complete and realistic assessment of this ghostly vision that is stressing me out so very much. I need to be in survival mode the same way I would if a predator was stalking me. But what or who is my predator? Could it be Lady Wrexham, as the local gossip suggests? Or it is a combination of tiredness and the excitement of being in a new place, with a spooky history that all add up to create this effect?

Tim woke suddenly as if there was an emergency, the declaration of an heroic siren, in this case, it was the sound of a very loud cockerel, who had decided to make the need for any wake-up alarm wholly redundant. Already wide awake, I looked around to make sure my knife wielding apparition was not about to pounce on me, before clambering over Tim to the bedroom window, grabbing hold of the curtain and pulling it aside in one strong fluid motion.

The light flooded in, bathing me in its warm golds, revealing the colours it had brought to the world beyond the window pane. I squinted at first until my eyes became accustomed to the light, there he was, the cockerel, the dominion of all birds strutting around outside, the sun igniting his brightly feathered plumes and his spirit for that matter, as he continued to squawk in the arrival of a new day with such admirable gusto.

Tim rolled over and caught hold of my nightie, pulling me backwards onto the bed, allowing me to fall unceremoniously on top of him, a ruse if ever there was one! He rolled me over and linked his fingers into my hand, shooting me a look that was all about sex with just the right hint of softness, he grabbed me again, more firmly than before, tighter like a vice. In that split second before he let his hands roam over me, every nerve in my body and brain became electrified, the anticipation of being together in a way that was more than words, a way that is so completely tangible.

Despite my lack of sleep and demonic encounters during the night, our morning antics had made me forget and brought a sense of peace to my world. The room was warm, I daren't tell Tim, he would tell me it was all my imagination, maybe it was, I would soon find out if it happened again tonight.

For now, we lay side by side, naked in the sunlight, the heat radiating over our bodies as if we were in a sauna, a warmth that invited a deep calming and restful feeling. We listened to the cacophony of birdsong, a flowing music that hydrated our parched souls. Tim's arm remained draped over my waist, I kissed his lips, I wanted this moment to last forever, he was such an amazing kisser, I gazed at the man I loved so much.

Tim glided his hand over the curves of my skin, there was a soft gentleness to his touch. "Have I ever told you I love you very much?" He whispered. I grinned, he said the exact same thing every time. "No, you haven't" I replied shaking my head and fighting away a grin that was trying to escape. Tim's hand migrated to my hair, pushing it away from my face. "Well, I do. And you know what?" folding my lips inwards so as not to speak, I heard the words before he even uttered them, "I always will, because you my darling, explode my monochrome world, into a rainbow wonderland." There was an intensity to his voice, his love was kerosene and I was his eternal flame, I loved it!

Eventually we got up, rummaged through the cardboard boxes marked 'Bedroom' that we had brought upstairs yesterday to find something to wear. For some unknown reason there was a box of cereal marked 'eat me!' amid the undies, which was a Bertie-bonus.

Breakfast was obviously the cereal and decaffeinated coffee, so naturally I had three cups as Tim laid the plans across the old wooden table which sat in the centre of the kitchen, "Ok, idea number one is Ziggy's bar for lunch," he said scanning the layout of the grounds and cottages. I looked puzzled, surely we should be getting on with things and not galavanting out for lunch? Tim decided to justify his comment. "Its a good place for food and hopefully we can find some of our much needed workforce there." Oh now I get it, I nodded in agreement, he was so resourceful but then he would be in his line of work. "Yes, good thinking, if we time it right Blot or Mogsey, the fishermen will be there and they are definitely a good source of local gossip and go-to for getting things done, nothing is secret, when you tell them, you tell the world and they have many connections."

Tim smiled, taking my arm as we negotiated our way over and around boxes and furniture in the orangery to the outside. Between the paving stones of the once pristine patio, weedy blooms so bold and tall tried to break free from their clumps and roam uninvited to areas where they were least expected to go and certainly not needed.

I looked up, releasing a heartfelt sigh, the weeds had even managed to wrap themselves around the drainpipe in their quest to climb and bloom, their petals smiling at us in the new day saying, 'you can't catch me!' Tim squeezed my arm, "Better get a gardener soon, much higher and they will be across the roof and down the other side," he joked. He wasn't wrong there, but I have to say the weeds were the least of our troubles.

The garden had evolved unhindered during the recent years of neglect with a few areas that were not too bad and others completely wild and overgrown, two extremes right next to one another, each one trying their best to enhance each other. Unfortunately, I am to gardening what Tim is to tidying, I see what's there but I don't have the slightest idea where to start or what to do. In truth, I have only ever taken sole responsibility for caring for a pot plant.

My mother had given me a small spider plant cutting and despite my lack of care, it turned into a monster that knew no bounds, as if it had been fed by some iron rich forest soil, rather than the dirty sand in an old plastic pot. The plant with its elongated, stripy leaves decided to take up residence across the width of my cupboard and trailed from the cupboard top to the floor and beyond. To stop the damn thing from tumbling over, I had to anchor it with string and nails. Luckily and with no help from me, it developed some strange orange growths which turned the leaves brown, causing it to die a premature death.

We continued to stroll around amidst the weeds, planning, evaluating and pointing out what needed to be done. Carefully listening and considering each others responses, that were built on empathy and logic, rich in a creative perspective taking, rather than reactive ramblings about the amount of work involved, it wasn't helpful and we already knew that!

We came across a tree that had probably once been the jewel of the garden, now it stood neglected and was in no state to be the jewel of anything apart from a large bonfire. The bark had a sort of creeping mildew and the leaves were curled and dried brown in an unhealthy way. Goodness, so many plants and weeds growing close to each other, in all fairness you couldn't really see what was plant and what was weed. We really did need to find either the previous gardener, whoever he was, or someone new. We would be able to get that information at Ziggy's too, we needed someone to potter, well, more that potter, we needed some creative magic working here.

By the time we had explored the garden, distillery and mill house it was already lunchtime. Luckily for me, we had run short of time so would have to leave the stone outhouses, scattered buildings and the old gatehouse for another day, phew, what a relief, I had been dreading that moment. I knew Tim would be by my side but it meant going inside one of the old stone buildings where I had been held hostage by Lord Wrexham and that was not something I relished at all. We made our way back inside the house and locked up before driving to Ziggy's bar.

CHAPTER 15

Ziggy's bar remained the epitome of the mellow Caribbean vibe, a distillation of sun, sand, rum and reggae and with it came all the untamed personalities of the Island that make life 'simply the best' to quote Tina Turner! Basically it is a large shed, constructed predominantly of driftwood and stuffed into some of its cracks are odds and sods which merge, creating its ambience and atmosphere.

The unmentionables are anything from bras, panties, socks, tobacco packets, to old fishing nets and weathered buoys, there was even an old Hoover hung up which someone had donated! The tables were simple round tin trays on legs constructed of iron rods curled at the base, rising upwards in a somewhat organic fashion, each one sat disorderly with plastic chairs that quite possibly could have been nicked from anywhere.

It was the 'go to' place on the Island for locals and over the years it had become a hotspot for tourists too. Often it was a place they had come across whilst visiting and liked the vibe and local amusement. Despite appearances the atmosphere is fantastic, it is a little piece of hidden paradise, although not for long, as it has now somehow made its way into the 'Hitchhikers Guide to the Caribbean' as one of the top ten places to hang out. Not sure it deserves that much accreditation but it is definitely worth a look.

The bar is run by Ziggy who came to the Island from Jamaica, he has a great personality with more magic in his a soul than you could ever realise it was possible to wish for. Nothing was ever a problem for him. Money would come, today was more important than a hundred tomorrows. He would always say, "Today is given, tomorrows are only a concept." Everyone is "dude" to him, everyone is his friend and judgement isn't his thing. He slides effortlessly between social groups and proudly wears the biggest afro hairstyle on the Island. He is proud to hold that record, it is a kind of artisanal topography that invites a sensual touch from many a tourist.

Luckily for us, ever the dependable Blot and Mogsey were both there, propping up the bar, nodding to the music, chatting and watching people drink, jump, sing and dance to the blaring reggae beats which attacked our ears from a sound system the size of an American home freezer. We paused for a couple of seconds to take in the spectacle, we also needed to accustom our noses and heads to the marijuana scent which wafted through the air. Maybe we should give the world some of this cool scent, could it help lead it to peace and a greater healing?

We caught Blot's eye and he waved us over, his arms flaying in all sorts of directions, like a demented octopus. "Welcome bac, Wah a yuh up tuh Hab yuh both moved tuh Iberville yet?" he slurred, "yeah man, that's what we have come about, we need some favours." Tim replied raising his eyebrows as Ziggy ambled over and lent over the bar, he loved to be part of any conversation. We each ordered a carib beer and some coconut dumplings, if we ate at the same time it would help soak up the beer and the hazy tint that caused our senses and heads swim from the sweet smell of marijuana. If we didn't eat I would tumble into a giddy darkness the sort that brings the most ridiculous joy as my mind enjoys the heady ride and would probably make a complete spectacle of myself in the process!

We caught up on all the latest gossip whilst earwigging in on many other conversations told in loud voices, as everyone tried to compete with the reggae beat that dominated the bar. Tim and I managed to gain control of the situation and began to reveal our plans whilst we had the attention of the locals. Tim cleared his voice from the smoke circling in front of him, usually it was Leroy who lurched into sermons but not on this occasion.

I glanced out at the beach and something caught my eye, I stared momentarily before Tim nudged me. Surely not, I rubbed my eyes, but the image of woman wearing a soaking-wet evening dress was still there, floating along the shore, her cries echoing over the waves. I really needed to get a grip before I sent myself crazy, it was tiredness that was all. Just as she had appeared, she disappeared, this was utter madness, I focused my attention back on Tim.

He was so handsome from the depth of his eyes to the gentle expressions of his voice. I loved the way his voice quickens when he sparkles with a new idea, he almost becomes lost in himself for a moment and quite forgets the mask he wears for others. So he began,"What we need is a workforce of socially and environmentally minded folks. They will be paid a comfortable live-in wage in return for helping us get the distillery, mill and exterior land plus the interior of Iberville up and running. There will be an additional offer of education and training for those wanting to stay on and work at the distillery. Every one of you can choose your preferred area of expertise, hopefully it will encourage and help all that want to learn new skills into a new area of work which in turn will help the Island's economy. We are convinced everyone has a skill they can offer and whatever they can bring to our project is good enough for us, we want Iberville to be a family, with enough love, nurture and care for everyone." Tim paused for a short breath and a quick glance around at the gathered local crowd before finishing, "It is a stepping stone into a fabulous future that will be thriving and ecologically sound for all of us."

It took a few seconds for the puzzled looks and open mouths to be absorbed and the spiel to sink it. "Basically we need help to renovate Iberville and get the distillery up and running again." I chirped, the bar on pause mode, as slowly their lips stretched wide into gaping grins, excitement glazed over their eyes, it was much more than their illegal substances having an effect, you could sense the magic welling from their souls as they wanted to help us. "Suh yuh waan wi tuh spread di word den?" Blot and Ziggy asked. Mogsey meanwhile, had already gathered a group of unsuspecting locals strolling by and had cornered them, shouting, "Yo man, there's jobs at Iberville wid Timmy an Jazzy Guh spill yuh yarn."

I'm not sure Tim liked being referred to as Timmy or being bashed across the back by Ziggy in his friendly manner, but what the hell, he took it all in his stride. We munched our way through a second lot of coconut dumplings which Ziggy brought as a type of trophy, whilst Blot rolled another spliff and talked incessantly about everything and nothing. Whatever point he was trying to make, it was littered with smiles and words and for us adopted Islander's, it was a real connection, flowing through us all, relaxed and full of love. You see why it's so easy to fall in love with the place, eventually we decided we had spent enough time getting not much work done and bid our fond farewells.

CHAPTER 16

We reached home via the minimart to collect much needed supplies and were greeted by a rather large gathering. There were people stood at the entrance, at the bottom of the drive and some had made their wait more comfortable by sitting on the steps of Iberville. Tim brought the car to an abrupt halt, we both looked at each other in complete astonishment, the Island grapevine was always good but I don't think either of us anticipated it to work quite so quickly or to attract quite so many people.

As we clambered out of the car laden with food bags, a sudden burst of energy came from the gathered crowd in the form of cheers and claps. We needed to get our shopping inside before the frozen items defrosted, but they had ideas of their own, vibrant clothes shining in the sunlight moving towards us like enchanting shoals of fish, chattering amongst each other.

It was chaotic that was for sure, but the hustle and bustle brought more life to Iberville, hopefully a sign of things to come. There was nothing for it but to go with the flow and move with the crowd. Tim signalled with his own special cavalier wave which meant I was to head to the orangery with the shopping whilst he would tackle the front entrance and keep the crowds amused. Unfortunately, best laid plans and all that, it didn't go according to plan, as some of the gathered crowd decided to follow me. Still at least there was enough of them to relieve me of my shopping bags.

As they followed, I felt slightly overwhelmed by the agglomeration of perfume, body odour accentuated by the mix of over-applied cologne. Somehow, despite the constant shouting I managed single handedly to herd them into the orangery as Tim held open the door smiling smugly as they all piled in. They were an eclectic bunch, but they all had one thing in common, from their faces came their true state. Their lines etched the story of a happy life but hard life, their crow's feet spoke of laughter and the deep creases in their cheeks told of people who gave away infinite smiles like they were wishes. My mother always told me to look at a persons face, it will tell you infinite things before any word is spoken. It's hard to imagine that there is truly a middle class when almost none of these people can afford to stay at home to raise their own children. It is a phenomenon seen for about two hundred years that the less well off are far more charitable, for one, they know the pain of poverty and hunger and they have no pretence of ongoing security so live in the reality of the moment, trying to make the best of each opportunity presented. And we had just delivered one!

This Island's community is vibrant with a strong society that is ready to nurture and protect anyone new comer. All of us need food, shelter, water and love and St kitts has always been ready to provide that welcoming hug to its visitors and Islanders alike.

We have all attempted at one time or another, to stand on the highest rung of the ladder and reach for the stars, whilst hacking away at the base of the same ladder. In todays society, taking care of the basics of life, the absolute essentials, is a noble cause to give ones life to, but it is the lack of respect for those professions and people that is the axe to the ladder. Take lack of respect for nature as an example, well it will bring an ecological catastrophe. Will the world ever choose to become a real community and see that love and respect for all, shown in emotional and practical ways is vital necessity for survival and not an optional add-on?

Sorry, I digress. Tim climbed onto one of the closed crates, that housed some of our smaller items of furniture and pulled me up beside him. This was our own stage and despite being extremely nervous, at this very moment there could be an audience of a million strong and I would be okay with that, because the only person I cared for was my number one fan standing next to me.

I would always be in his arms no matter where we were, right from that very first moment when we looked deeply into each other's eyes and felt that spark of passion. I could stand up and speak to anyone, anywhere in the world and it would be the same as sitting on my couch at home. That's what love can do, it can bring out the strongest version of you and shield you from the nonsense that can be thrown your way.

Tim cleared his throat as our hopeful audience became a silent sea of smiles, a chorus of quiet gentle hearts awaiting our beginning. I won't bore you all with the whole speech as it went on for at least twenty minutes, but suffice to say, a brief synopsis went along the lines of: Tim and I can improve the Islands standard of living and economy and bring together a real sense of family love, but in return anyone who comes to work here must come with a mutual respect and understanding. Tim and I want them all to feel safe and secure and enjoy the camaraderie and companionship of living and working together. At Iberville there will be a strong trust and hard work, any thoughts of power and obsession is for losers. We are always connected, each person has a valuable role to play. Tim went on to encourage everyone to speak to us with an idea of the roles they would like to take on and we would give them all consideration. They would learn on the job so to speak with tradesmen from the village who already possessed certain skills.

The long sermon seemed to work though, as he came to the end of his final sentence and paused for a breath, huge cheers rose into the air like the greatest of any celebratory firework explosion, Tim looked at me, winking and knowing he had pitched it just right. Language and culture are reflections of one another, that feed each other, for better or worse, in this day and age you have to take great care with the power of words. I grinned nervously back, I felt sick to the stomach but that is a good signal, it shows that I am at a new frontier that is exciting too, only through these travels can I truly unravel my talents and gifts.

Everyone suddenly surged forwards, each person wanting their chance to speak first and secure a job, unfortunately in the process, they managed to collide with the crate we were stood on. Whilst Tim held on to his composure, I of course lost mine, I moved like my knees were hinges, arms flapping in the air with no sense of timing, wobbling to and fro before falling backwards onto my bottom. Everyone clapped like it was all part of the plan as Tim helped me up again, pride not intact. Falling is always the easy part, gravity is an efficient force, it's dealing with the impact, getting back up with some decorum and feeling unashamed that is the real challenge. I wish I didn't blush so fast, but alas I don't seem to have the ability to keep my emotions to myself. In an instant my cheeks were a rosy blob of champagne for everyone to see.

Anyway, my fall was soon forgotten and by the time we had spoken to everyone, taken names and contact details so we could process it all, it was almost dark. I let out a slow controlled breath in an attempt to loosen my body, I was exhausted. I gave my shoulders a wiggle and lolled my head in a circle, I felt like I needed a hot bath, but that was on the to-do list so would be put on hold for now.

Tim looked at me, "Best I can do is sit you in a bucket of water for now." He laughed, mmhm that could be an option worth exploring! He continued, "My brain feels as if I have been on a treadmill and it needs to press stop." I nodded, also feeling an emotional pull towards lethargy as fatigue suddenly began to take hold, we have, after all, worked at full pelt this afternoon and this was only the beginning!

We have another long day ahead of us tomorrow, looking at all the applicants, looking at those who really have their heart set on working for us and those that don't. We also have to match the skilled tradesmen to the jobs we have available and find a perfect skill set and ambition for those who need to learn. It would take time and there would be disappointments along the way, but there was not enough work for everyone. Thats business for you, I do hope Tim doesn't want to interview them all after that!

Utterly exhausted we made our way upstairs to our bedroom collecting a hot drink and something to eat from one of the bags I had literally dumped in the fridge. Oh well, they weren't going anywhere, it was another day tomorrow so I will put them away after breakfast. Good job Tim and Leroy had managed to get the electrics in working order before we moved in! "We are not going to make a habit of this" Tim joked, "No definitely not, I have had enough of people already, let's become recluses for a few hours." I replied, he laughed, "No, no, I mean putting on our pyjamas and sitting in bed with socks on cradling warm drinks before we go to sleep, I can think of much better ways to unwind from the trials and tribulations of the day." I giggled as he pulled me under the duvet.

In the darkness of our room our tired fingers slowly caressed each other's skin as if we were afraid a heavier touch would break the heady magic. Despite our overwhelming tiredness, we became one, one mind with one goal and purpose, each utterly drunk with love for one another. A few moments later, it was all over and with a stretch and a yawn, we both fell asleep snuggled tightly together, he was my big spoon and I was his little spoon, this was our cocoon. This time, I slept, no nightmares awoke me.

CHAPTER 17

I was awoken once more to the sound of that damn cockerel, once I am awake there is no retreat. I stole a quick glance at the pointless alarm clock as the days tasks started to demand me to think about them, find solutions and get the jobs done.

Tim was already up and standing by the window dressed, looking at his watch, which resembled something beamed in from the "Starship Enterprise." One of his many spy gadgets that kept him on track and in touch with what was going on in their world. The down side of that was that at any time, a message or call could come through that often caused him to take a million random detours that would eventually eat up his day.

He strolled over to the bed and put his arms around me, instantly transporting me to a serene space once more, a place of loving restoration. "Jaz, darling, just taken a call from our handler, Leroy and I have to meet with him urgently. I really need to go, will you be ok, it should only be a couple of hours, we can carry on where we left off yesterday when I get back, ok?" I nodded, I knew this would happen, one of the not so good perks of being married to a spy. "Sure, you go, I will be fine." He stole a kiss from me, one steeped in passion, a promise of realness, of primal desire before pulling back and disappearing out of the room, clicking two fingers as if he was firing a gun, "Catch you later gorgeous," and with that he was gone. This was so annoying but I need to learn to have more patience and empathy, I knew this when I married Tim, after all perfection is boring!

However the one thing I did not have the patience for and was finding increasingly annoying was the cockerel. I got up, picked up my trainer and launched it out the window, in the hope of some respite from its incessant crowing. Luckily I am not a good shot and it missed him by a mile, as he continued to stride amongst the weeds as if it was his. Every worm in the buried soil was his for the taking and he was utterly focused on this pleasant game. His head moving as if he was part biological and part machine, lots of little cogs in that tiny neck. All in all he was a joyful fluff of feathers basking in the morning sun.

Breakfast was toast with peanut butter and a glass of oat milk, now I was all set up for the day ahead. I decided that whilst Tim was absent I would face my demons, I had to do it sometime as Iberville was now my home and I couldn't do much without him for the moment. When I say face my demons, what I mean is going back into the derelict stone out buildings that I was imprisoned in a fews years back. I was put there after attending a media shindig here and got too close to solving the murder and reporting the truth, so I needed to be silenced by those involved.

I made my way outside, through the neglected garden to the building I remembered so well. I stood in front of it, staring, motionless, my whole body shaking, then the first signs of the panic arrived, a discomfort in my chest, a feeling in my brain like I have had excess caffeine, as it sets in deeper. I feel the urge to run, escape, hide, but no I mustn't I must face this.

Our fears can be triggered by either real threats or by painful memories of threats, the trick is challenging ourselves to unlearn fears. Tim keeps telling me that when I am scared I must ask myself, how real is the threat, have I begun to generalise fear and seek only the evidence to cement it rather than challenge it. To do this I need to remain well balanced with a good perspective, I need to take action to protect myself. In summary, my fears can be real, ghosts of real fears, or entirely imagined, but it takes courage to figure them out and face them. I do appreciate that it takes courage to face your fears, but it is worth it, Tim would say it was, so I needed to do this.

I took a step forwards, panic began to override the need to move, I really need to find the confidence to keep walking. The difference between taking this step forwards or not, is everything, it will define who I am. I took some deep breaths and gave myself a stern talking, "I am right here, I am safe and protected , this is my own home, the past cannot hurt me now." It seemed to work slowing down the messages of panic and giving my brain a chance to become focused and put me back in the driver's seat once more. I am strong, I am not going to become stressed or let my actions become erratic and escalate further, engulfing me and cause me to do something stupid.

Right! Best foot forward, I made my way into the tunnel, shorter than I remember, until I arrived at the dreaded door. Then with great difficulty managed to move it open, there was no way it was going to close in a hurry, the door would probably fall apart first, it was full of woodworm. I took a deep breath, peered in and then stepped inside, nothing had changed, it was like stepping back in time. The iron bed was still there, the old pillow and scratchy green blanket laying abandoned on it. A shaft of light highlighted shadows as it forced its way through the slit in the stone wall.

I didn't venture too far, in fact I stood pretty much next to the open door, my heart pounding in my chest, despite my trying to stay in control. But I didn't did I? Stay in control I mean. I let out the most almighty scream that came from a terror, lost in absolute fear of the most desperate form.

The scream was primal, right from my mouth and the bottom of my lungs. I stood there, my back to the stone wall, the roughness pressing into my skin. Sounds started to arrive in my brain from afar, but my touch somehow disconnected, my eyes seeing picture perfectly, without the use of any recreational chemicals, as in front of me slowly appeared a fog condensed into the shape of an apparition. At first it was weird, it had no surrounding form, but then it evolved into a woman from beyond the world of eyes. A lady, dressed in a flowing white and blue gown. Still initially faint but becoming clearer as the form morphed into a person, who looked like they would be quite capable of moving matter in our world, she was glowing, smiling and rubbing her hands together.

I wanted to emit another scream but this time, despite my efforts, no sounds would emerge from my mouth, instead my eyes fell downwards to the apparitions' feet, as the foggy envelope appeared to be melting and forming tiny puddles of water. A cold wind tickled the back of my neck causing me to shudder, the rays of sunlight that highlighted the stone walls began to flicker and a soft voice whispered in my ear. "At last my darling, Jaz, this has taken an absolute age. I've missed you, but now we have found each other, we are going to have the best time. Oh and I need you to help me."

I jerked my head to one side and swallowed hard as I heard a strangled cry rent the air that I recognised as my own voice. The female figure moved in front of me, rubbing her electric blue hands together, "Please Jaz, please, this is going to be a great journey." She began to whimper like a lost child, clutching at a rag doll which had now magically appeared in her arms. As I continued to try and work out who this was, the whimpering turned to a giggle as she began to clap her hands and laugh like she had seen something funny. I stood frozen to the spot trying to make any sense or get a grasp of the situation.

Eventually I managed to move, speak and control my fear, after all how can I be scared of the dead when the living are so volatile? I blinked as she stared right back at me, now her demeanour had changed, she had a look of hurt and buried pain, as if she feared being vulnerable more than the reality of actually being dead. I reached out my hand, trembling, it passed straight through her, "LLLL…ady Amélie WWW… rexham? I stammered, she stared back before agreeing, "Yes that is I, you saved me at the beach when I was caught in that awful net, remember?" My brain stuttered for a moment as every part of me tried to come out of pause mode and let my thoughts catch up.

After a minute or two I stepped forward, "This is utter madness, what is going on, all these visions and noises, was that you, why can I see you, you are dead aren't you?" Lady Amélie went to place her hand on my shoulder, but despite my retraction backwards she was unable to touch me. "Jaz, call me Amélie, you are correct in both assumptions. Yes, to all of your questions, I am deceased and yes you can see me as we have a special connection. Don't be afraid, I needed to reach out and get you to notice me. I have selected you to help me, I want to learn how to feel loved and begin to love myself and to find some justice so I can complete my journey home to rest forever, please say you will help me as you have before."

CHAPTER 18

This was just weird enough, talking to the ghost of Amélie, who would believe me. She continued, " I can't rest and depart from this world until I am at peace with the choices I made in my living years and understand how I met my untimely demise. I need you to help me find justice."
I think I can understand how she feels, anyway I wanted to get out of here in 'tout suite' fashion, so I just nodded in agreement. "I will be in touch soon." Amélie muttered as I grimaced, was this for real?

My life has taken lots of twists and turns since coming to the Caribbean but never in my life did I ever think I would experience a paranormal exchange. A sort of telephone exchange for those who wish to talk to the living and who believe in ghosts. Imagine if this got out, I would be the laughing stock of the Island.

I turned to walk out of the door, but something made me glance back, she was gone, nowhere to be seen, it was as if the encounter never happened. I felt a cold breeze blow past me as I put my hand on the stone wall, trying to pull the door shut, no idea why, we would be pulling it down soon. The stone was absolutely freezing cold to the touch, if I left my hand there for too long, I suspect it would become stuck, so I left the door ajar and made my way back up the tunnel to daylight once more.

As I came out of the tunnel I heard shots being fired nearby, my nerves were already frazzled so, now fearing for my life, I dived forward and crouched behind one of the bushes, trying to peer through to see what was going on whilst remaining hidden. I had had plenty of practise at this art but as I hit the dusty ground I felt a sneeze brewing, I couldn't give away my hiding place!

Trying to contain the sneeze to a quieter, more delicate sound, I became aware of a pair of eyes peering through the shrubbery at me. It was the ghost of Amélie crouched in front of me, maybe this was for real. "What do you think you are doing?" I whispered to her. "Same as you, hiding from whoever is shooting at us." This was utter madness, why on earth was I talking to a ghost that may or may not exist depending on what my imagination was trying to conjure up?

I heard Tim's shouts nearby, thank goodness he had returned just in the nick of time, but then his timing was always impeccable. Wait, if I let him know where I am, I could get us both killed. Mmhm, what to do? My eyes darted around looking for anything that could be a secret signal to him alone. Luckily an empty coconut husk lay on the ground within a hands reach, I grabbed it and then did a jack in the box manoeuvre as I lobbed it over the top of the shrub, hoping and praying that my astute secret agent would put two and two together and come to my rescue. Luckily for me, he did. "He has seen it, he is coming." Amélie announced clapping her hands before disappearing into the ether.

Tim pulled me out of the bushes and sat next to me on the grass as I surveyed the surrounding area. There was nothing of course! "Dare I even ask what you have been up to?" He asked grinning and removing bits of twigs and leaves from my hair.

I'm ashamed to say before replying I took one of the leaves from Tim's hand and wiped my nose. "lovely" was all he said. "Well, I decided to conquer my fear of that building where I told you I was held hostage and…" I blurted out but then stopped in my tracks," and what?" Tim asked. If I carried on, I would run the risk of being the source of ridicule for quite sometime to come, I was sure of that.

Tim held my gaze."Come on tell me, you can't leave it mid sentence, if it makes it easier for you, I love you and that will never change, what happened in there? Tell me." Promise me you won't laugh at me"came my reply. "Promise, now spill those beans Mrs Meyers" he answered putting his fingers to his head swearing allegiance with a scouts salute. "I met Lady Amélie's ghost, we talked and she wants me to help her with something before she can rest and then she disappeared. Then when I came out, I heard gunshots so I hid in the shrubbery, thats it really." I answered, trying hard to make it all seem so very normal!

After an awkward moment he gave out a huge guffaw of laughter followed by a sucking in of his cheeks and then wiped a rogue tear of laughter from his eye. The corner of Tim's mouth twitched, if there was a world leader-board for smirkers, he'd be champion. Eventually he stopped laughing enough to say, "Lady Amélie's ghost and guns shots, oh Jasmine!" Have you been at the cleaning fluid again, there is nothing and no one else here, you imagined it, what did you have for breakfast?" "Peanut butter on toast, why?" Well, there you are, it's the additives playing havoc with your psyche." I knew this was only to be scoffed at, even I was not entirely convinced by my ghostly encounter.

Anyhow, it was still rude, but I laughed it off as he took my hand and gave it a gentle squeeze, "Come on, before your imagination runs completely amok and you start seeing little furry animals," he uttered helping me up off the grass. Together we ambled back into the house for some respite from the heat. Despite his comments and my uncertainty, I can promise you that it was definitely not my imagination. There were three of us on that amble, Amélie walked beside us pulling faces at Tim, why was it only me that could see her, why had she chosen me?

CHAPTER 19

For the rest of that day Tim and I were kept busy with the hustle and bustle and organisation of locals that we had hired, all of them coming and going with tools, equipment and much needed materials. Our carpenter Benni, or Bench as he was aptly named by his friends was amazing to watch, he set to work straight away, he was a builder and an artist, he would also be a great teacher to those who wanted to learn the trade.

As I watched, sometimes he was lifting several planks of timber onto his shoulders and effortlessly carrying them off ready to make some vast structures and at other times he was absorbed in the finest details of his plans. He was akin to a chef that savours every drop, keen to use all that nature has given so graciously. You could tell that he had the heart and the hands to honour wood and give its beauty a new life.

Iberville came to resemble a building site in a very short space of time, it is and will be a place of caution for a while as hopefully together, we will make steady progress. From its foundations, amid the machines and the people who labour, a whole new world will open up to Iberville, although I have to say a digger wasn't the first tool I thought we would need.

But it trundled past us, buttercup yellow, kissed with earth on its caterpillar tracks.

It wasn't until almost the end of the day when Tim and I were alone that I remembered about his meeting with his handler. He hadn't mentioned it, I know he has to adhere to confidentiality but surely he would have said it went well or something along those lines. I had been so wrapped up in the stupid ghost thing, that I forgot to ask him about it. "Tim, I am so sorry darling, I forgot to ask how the meeting went this morning," I asked him as we prepared supper. "Oh yes, good thanks, I am still in gameful employment, there is a reasonably high chance Leroy and I will need to go under cover for a month or so." I put the saucepan full of pasta on to boil, "Oh, ok, will that be soon, anything exciting?" I asked.

Tim nodded, putting down the knife he had been using to chop up vegetables, "Potentially, for about a week now, Venezuela has been in the grips of a political battle between President Maduro and the opposition leader Juan Guaido, you know, the politician and member of the social-democratic party who has been in the news." "Oh yes," "Well at the moment dozens of other countries recognise him as the country's legitimate head of state, but Maduro has started to fight back with his own regime's, saying he is the one in power. He has recently deployed various air defence assets illegally. So we are going to be placed out there with a few others to assess the situation and help to prevent any possible war if we can." Crikey, these spies really do land themselves in some scrapes but he can look after himself and save the backs of others at the same time, I don't doubt. "I will be on tender-hooks until you get back safely, when do you go?" I asked. "No firm dates as yet but it could just be a phone call at any time, don't worry, it will all be fine and I will be back before you have had time to miss me, contact may need to be quite infrequent." He grinned. It was a pain him having to go, but we always knew it was on the cards, I could manage and so could Goldie.

We dusted off the table yet again and sat down to eat as Amélie appeared from out of nowhere, "Ca a l'air assez bon à manger." She uttered in French. I looked up startled, and waved my hand in the air as if to shoo her away. "Are you ok, or do you have some new tic you need to tell me about?" Tim asked. I smirked, "Yes sorry it's just that the …" "ghost umm, what's her name, Amélie has reappeared." He butted in mocking me. "Actually yes, you can't see her then?" Tim shook his head and began to titter which soon turned into great waves of stomach holding hilarity. "I wasn't joking, seriously Tim, she is here, standing right next to me now actually."

Tim looked around with his hand to his head as if he was searching, "Nope, definitely can't see her, let me take a swipe." He swept his arm through the air as Amélie ducked out of the way before beginning to add her four-penny worth to the conversation, "Tell him I am real, he nearly hit me. I will prove to him that I am real by," she paused thinking for a moment. "Mmhm, I will move his plate across the table and throw his glass into the air." I giggled childishly despite my adult years, like she could do that. Tim regained his composure and took a mouthful of pasta, "Honestly Jaz, we will have to get you committed, if you carry on like this, there is no such thing as ghosts, it's all in your over-active imagination." Was it, could I see her or was it my imagination, maybe if I could find a way to make him see what I can see, then we would be able to tell if she was really there or not.

Without any warning Tim shouted "Boo." Completely not expecting that, both Amélie and I jumped. Tim placed his hand on my arm "For goodness sake Jaz, it was a joke, you really are quite twitchy." He grinned as I gave him one of my looks that said I wasn't impressed by his antics. Amélie in the meantime, had retreated and was standing behind me like some scared kitten. How the hell can a ghost be scared? I smiled to myself as she disappeared through the wall in disgust, at least I knew one way to get rid of her!

I suppose all Amélie ever wanted was for someone to hear her, see her, to heal her even. She had rarely been heard or seen in her living years, unaccustomed to any form of love and so in death she had no way of seeing heaven's gate, well not yet anyway. She apparently had 'things to do before passing on and I was her pass to put right what was wrong,' I suppose it was so important to her that she had been given more time from her maker. Amélie was alive and dead at the same time, perhaps what some might call an angel.

Tim and I cleared away the plates, put on some easy listening music and danced our way up the staircase into the sanctuary of our bedroom, the only place where we could forget about what was going on. It was yet another day where tiredness won its battle and we soon fell asleep snuggled close to each other. Falling asleep was fast becoming one of the best parts of the day, beneath our cozy sheets, so snug and safe, we could let reality leave us and let the world of dreams come in.

Still with Amélie on my mind, I dreamt of a young rich girl playing and singing hymns with her sister. She went to bed alone that night but her maid was awoken by a scuffle she thought she heard. The young girl staggered into the kitchen and cried, "I am stabbed, I am stabbed in the heart. She died instantly, despite the frantic efforts of the maid to save her. As her father began to investigate the death of his beloved daughter, he found out that she had been stabbed by her fiancé, for having an illicit affair with his father. The fiancé ended up being committed to a Lunatic Asylum as he made out that some strange alien from out of space killed her.

CHAPTER 20

I woke suddenly, not because of any noise or interruption, but because my dream seemed to have come to an abrupt conclusion. My night movie had ended, credits had rolled and it was time to engage in the real world once more.

It was just getting light, I rolled over and snuggled into Tim who was still fast asleep, or so I thought! As I nestled in blowing into his ear, with one swift movement he rolled over and pulled me close to him, running his hands up my bare arms, not slow but fast, sending a surge of electricity through me. His manly hands began to roam all over my skin, his soft lips following in quick succession. To be in these arms is love, safety, and passion all rolled into one. This morning I was going to get my way, I rolled on top of him and of course, one thing led to another and bam, it didn't end until our bodies were still once more, very warm and as close as two souls could be. What a great way to start the day!

Just as I thought the day couldn't get any better, the predictable phrase came, "have I ever told you I love you? Blah blah" he uttered, I grinned, "as I do you, you know you always say that after we have you know…." I started to say but ended the sentence with, "What the hell do you think…." Tim looked completely bewildered for a second before realising the situation. "Oh my God, it's your damn thing, ghost or whatever she is, she is here, isn't she?"

Before I could reply he quickly retrieved the sheets to maintain some dignity for both of us. It's not like him to be shy, does this mean he believes me now? I nodded and shouted sternly into thin air, "Amélie, not the bedroom, this is private, have you no shame, you mustn't come in here, right?" Tim laughed, "She is going to be a right pain in the ar…," "Tim, thats enough, she can hear you" He looked at me slightly shocked before finishing with something like "you look like a total loony talking to the end of the bed." "J'ai entendu, j'irai mais c'est aussi ma maison" Amélie replied, "was your house, now get out" I answered crossly as she disappeared through the wall once more dejected and continuing to mumble some random words in French. Despite having a French O'level, I had no idea what she was ranting on about!

Tim and I gathered our senses before making our way downstairs. Our workforce had already arrived and were in full swing, when I say that, I do not mean on the work front! My dilapidated kitchen was even more of a complete mess, if that was in any way possible. They had helped themselves to almost everything and anything they could find to eat and drink. Amid it all was Amélie, sat cross legged amongst the debris scattered on the table, urging them on, I only hope no-one can see her. "Oh for gods sake, look at this mess, Tim."

As the mess grew with them completely oblivious to us standing there, my anxiety grew too.

Tim, sensing the sheer frustration in my voice cleared his throat and began speaking, almost burning with hot words not sugar coating anything. Although his temper can be fiery, that may do more damage and we don't want them to walk out before they have even started. The crowd fell silent then came a lot of apologising. He turned to face me, "Well that won't be happening again" he smirked as he started to help me clear up the mess and in doing so swept Amélie off of the table, I giggled, as Tim ignored it and commented, "Let's not be too strict with them, it's not often you see everyone or anyone so keen to be working in the Caribbean." He was right and the last thing I wanted to do was to stop any productivity!

With that Benji and another guy, who introduced himself as Dix arrived. "Come see dude, we have a surprise for you." They led the way into the drawing room, well I was speechless, it was totally beautiful, walls plastered ready to paint, polished wooden floors and neat trims, what they had done was utterly fabulous. "I know we are working outside too, but you have been good to us and we wanted to do another room for you, so we all worked really late." Dix said. Both men looked pleased with themselves and so they should be. Ok so you can sort of forgive the current mess when they do things like that can't you? I flung my arms around them initiating a hug of gentle arms that still gave us all the space to breathe but showing them that there is no finer praise.

From the slightly cleared patio we became aware of a disorganised hammering noise followed by a few choice swear words. On further investigation, Goldie and Leroy were outside on some seemingly DIY kick. "What on earth?" I asked as they stood amidst an array of differing lengths of wood. I didn't want to appear too rude as their project hadn't really progressed well enough to know what it was going to be.

Tim and I glanced at each other, each trying to come up with possibilities, whatever it was, I do hope it was for them. Goldie took my arm and lead me back into the house, whilst Tim began conversing with Leroy. "We are making a coffee table for our lounge," she grinned, "lovely idea, it's going to look great," I replied. What had once been brightly coloured doors, from a neighbourhood where fuchsia and sky-blue were common was now in the throws of becoming something quite different, artistic in its own way. In the wood grain there were still streaks of colours, creams, blues and greens too. I sort of liked it for being reclaimed, made perfect by all those random imperfections, but grateful that this creation would not be coming anywhere near Iberville!

As I walked Goldie through to the drawing room to show her what the guys had done she squealed with excitement, "Mi hab spoken tuh fi mi uncle an he a happy tuh train wi tuh becum private investigators buh wi need ah name." This was great news, although I did expect her to squeal more about the new room than her uncle training us. Her uncle, the commissioner, only took on the most gifted people who were willing to toil and produce a high standard of work, it would be a hard road to becoming a private investigator he would make sure of that. The price paid would not be in money but blood, sweat and many a few tears. Not entirely convinced that this was one of my best career moves I asked, "Do you think we are ready to be locked and loaded," Goldie giggled, "thats fi wi name Locked and loaded." And so thats what happened.

CHAPTER 21

Over the next six months or so the renovations continued at Iberville and Goldie and Leroy started work with a project of their own to make my old shack their home. Our training to become private investigators commenced and went full steam ahead, luckily Tim and Leroy's big mission was put on hold as the Venezuelan crisis seemed to die down, although it still smouldered away in the background ready to explode into a political war at anytime.

Tim and Leroy still had work closer to home, their operations never revealed. Real-world espionage rarely resembles the on-screen exploits of movie secret agents. Instead it is a useful and often dangerous way for governments to gather information about real and potential enemies. The successes and failures of spies have shaped foreign policy, altered the course of wars and left a deep (though usually hidden) impression on world history. World leaders are faced with making important decisions every day, and information is the key to them making the right decision. How many troops does your enemy have? How far are they in developing their secret weapons? Are they planning to negotiate a trade deal with another country? However whilst some of this intelligence may be readily available, most countries keep their most valuable information that could be used against them well hidden. Tim says that in order to gain access to secret information, governments use espionage, a blend of subterfuge, deception, technology, data analysis and also use similar tools to counteract the spying efforts of the enemy or to feed them false information.

Quick lesson in espionage over. Amélie, had become our resident ghost and for the most part kept her temper so long as no-one disturbed her picture that hung in the hallway. It was a hideous portrait blackened by age and didn't even resemble her anymore. She practised the art of disappearing and reappearing through walls until she became proficient at it, appearing at the most inopportune moments. I think Tim gave up trying to persuade me she didn't exist and instead just put up with me talking to thin air on many occasions.

At least Goldie believed me, luckily for her Amélie decided to reveal herself and allegedly gave her the power of paranormal sight too, as Amélie called it. Anyway after an initial clash of personalities, they seemed to accept each another, especially when Amélie helped Goldie find her lost keys. Our pain in the preverbal ghost also found that she had developed powers which enabled her to touch and move things, it drove me insane sometimes, especially when I could have sworn I put an item in a specific place and Amélie moved it, giggling churlishly to herself. If that wasn't enough, Amélie had a tendency to speak French at any given moment, irritating me to no end which she enjoyed. What with her and

Goldie it was a wonder I ever managed to get a hold of conversations, I learnt how to ignore it for the most part.

On the private investigator front, it was so much more than we had ever expected, physically and emotionally demanding. Somehow through all the mess our aim was to create a kind of order in which good stories could become a reality in more people's lives and help to the rest become consigned to history.

The training scenarios we were given were hard and often heartbreaking, some not having the outcomes you would want. Still it would stand us in good stead, a good private investigator will see the clues and logic and is able to immerse themselves in the emotional complexity of the social ether and start to make life better for their clients and the local community.

Goldie's uncle had given us a covert operation as one of our tests. Initially we were both excited, there wasn't anything cooler than being asked to go on stakeout. I had heard Tim talk of it often, on this occasion he just laughed at us when we both turned up for our task wearing dark clothes and sunglasses. Trying to look inconspicuous we strolled through the park completing our surveillance, even managing to get a breakfast sandwich whilst watching these idiots.

This surveillance job was a piece-of-cake, what could possibly go wrong? We did our homework beforehand doing background checks. Our task was basically to gather evidence using observation and tracking techniques on a fake employee who had a recent record of absenteeism. After five hours of surveillance, bored does not begin to express the feelings we felt, but our investigations revealed that this employee was committing fraud, using corporate credit cards for unauthorised purchases. We passed with flying colours, with a gentle reminder to complete the paperwork side of things afterwards.

Despite some areas of the job likely to be tedious, being private-eye's would suit us very nicely. Once we qualified we could do things our way, no one ever follows the law to the letter, how boring! Most criminals are scary nut-jobs anyway, so we need to be able to get leverage on them and sometimes that might mean being slightly under-hand.

As time progressed Goldie and I seemed to have quite the knack for our new business venture, in some ways our background in Journalism had stood us in good stead. We helped get a few bad guys locked up with Goldie's uncle by our side coaching us, offering a time honoured way through murky waters, a sort of Dante-esque tour through the hell of criminality.

Eventually the day came when we passed out and collected our badges proving we now had the skills to solve the crimes alone and more importantly, the emotional pull to find the culprits, no matter the cost. We were so happy. 'Locked and Loaded Private Investigators' really were locked, loaded and ready to take on the world!

Tim and Leroy were so proud of us and to show us how much they took us to an upmarket restaurant where we all celebrated. Dix, one of our workers spread the word around Iberville and beyond, letting all know that we were ready to make a positive difference in the world. In Tim's words, "You have both risen to become voices for society and have found strength in your identity as women." Why can't he just say he was proud!

Qualifying couldn't have come at a better time as Tim and Leroy were sent away on a mission as the Venezuelan crisis he had talked about previously came to a head. From the small snippets they were able to tell us, I was able to glean that many people were protesting and had been arrested for wanting what they thought were fair demands. They were of course met with repression as the security forces responded to the protests by firing tear gas and rubber bullets.

Digging deeper as they do, senior officials managed to detect numerous cases of barbaric killings, torture, violence and underhand disappearances against anyone who criticised the government. Agents were sent to infiltrate and investigate crimes committed on a large-scale targeting innocent civilians, regardless of their nationality. Venezuela's illegitimate president, Mr Maduro blamed the country's dire economic state on the protests imposed by imperialism. It sounded all very complicated and a complete mess, I wouldn't want to be in the middle of it.

Iberville had now become a working distillery and was on the way to become a large scale global exporter. The cottages had been renovated into homes for those working on the estate and the garden had become pristine once again, which meant the house renovation could really take off. Luckily Tim and I had gone through all our plans with the builders prior to his posting so that they knew what needed to be done and carry on without much input from us.

CHAPTER 22

I didn't sleep well on this particular night, I think it was being alone at Iberville for the first time and the unnerving tranquility from Amélie, she had been absent for far too long.

Just as I was thinking about her, I heard a clicking noise, someone or something was behind the bedroom door. It couldn't be Amélie as she would come through the wall or up through the floor. Sweat started to trickle down my neck and I crept further under the duvet, my breath quickening as the door creaked open but everything was silent just an unnerving darkness. What was I doing I was a private detective, trained for all eventualities, not to hide like some frightened rabbit!

I peered out from the sheets and saw a light strobe then a glimpse of a figure moving awkwardly back and forth across the room. "Amélie is that you?" I called out in a confident questioning manner, anyone who wanted to take me on, would come a cropper, I would make sure of that despite feeling vulnerable. "Oh good, you are here, I couldn't see you, it's too dark" came her reply. Breathing a sigh of relief I turned the light on, slightly irritated by her appearing act. "What the hell are you doing here at this time of the morning and what possessed you to scare me like that opening the door? Can't you come through the wall anymore?" "I didn't want to scare you and I wanted to see if I could open things. Also its the middle of the night, ghosts don't sleep, I got bored of walking through walls," she answered very matter of fact.

By now she had made herself comfortable and was lying next to me, "You didn't answer what you were doing here?" I asked her. "Tilly has been in the house and stolen my locket" she replied. I lay there staring into the darkness, explanations of most aspects of life can only make real sense if they sound intelligent and this was not, Tilly was dead we all watched her drown. "Amélie, this is ridiculous I watched her die in Anegada, she drowned and there have been no sightings of her since. How on earth do you know she has been in the house? And, could this not have waited until the morning?" Wailing like a banshee, she shouted, "I'm telling you she has trespassed in our house again, I smelt her and she has taken my locket, I want it back."

I could feel the sandman come heavy to my eyelids, the shuttering of my synapses wanting to lure me to sleep, each limb becoming heavy, my heart slowing to a more peaceful beat, "Amélie, this is ridiculous, you didn't see her, how can you smell her and how do you know your locket has gone? I need to sleep we will continue this in the morning, now go and haunt someone else." I yawned and rolled onto my side,

"Que Dieu vous damne mortels" was the last sentence I heard her utter as I closed my eyes.

As I came to, I became aware of heated voices, I got up and dressed in record time, before going downstairs to witness Goldie having a discussion with, to any unassuming onlooker, herself in the great hall, what she was actually doing was conversing with the rather stressed and animated ghost of Amélie. There was no heat in her voice, she was just taking a different view of things and advising on different ways of doing things. Amélie balked at first, she was unaccustomed to not getting her way. Goldie had got used to her fiery temper as had I and we learnt how to absorb things, responding rather than reacting, It seemed to work in calming the situations rather than add to the anger of the ghost.

Goldie caught sight of me and raised her eyebrows, "Amélie thinks Tilly broke into Iberville and has stolen her locket, she smelt her presence!" she said trying not to laugh, "I know I had the same conversation with her in the wee small hours of this morning." I replied exasperated that this was still ongoing. "When you two have finished mocking me, I am here you know." Amélie interjected. Before she had a chance to launch into a conversation, there was a knock at the front door. I opened it to reveal Mogsey, gosh something serious must have happened, he never came to anyone's house. "Hi Mogsey, Come in, come in, are you ok?" I asked as his eyes began to dance robotically from side to side whilst surveying the place. "Mi ave ah job fah locked an loaded, awon hav stolen fi mi boat an fishing gear."

Goldie and I walked Mogsey into the drawing room and sat him down with a coffee, "Anyting eena dis?" He asked pointing at the coffee. "No, just coffee, can you tell us exactly what has happened? I asked, looking around for a pencil and paper to in order to take notes, Goldie was already one step ahead and took out a notepad and pen from her shorts pocket, as Mogsey began. "Well Mi gaan tuh git fi mi boat dis mawning afta buying bait fram Blot an ih did gaan. Nuh eena eh usual place an fi mi mawning rope did hav bin cut. Thats ih fi mi lively hood gaan Nuh fish Mi cyaan nyam. can yuh fine fi mi boat quickly?"

Goldie and I nodded as we listened intently, "Told you, it was Tilly, she has come back from the dead, stolen the boat and my locket" Amélie piped up, "Shhh" I said. Mogsey gave me an odd stare unsure whether he should continue or not, "No, no, not you, sorry, please go on." I urged him, the last thing I wanted was to become the butt of many jokes, if I tried to explain about the ghost that was sat next to him. "Thats ih, nutten else tuh tell, Ih did stolen overnight sometime" Mogsey replied.

At this point in the proceedings we usually need to ask further questions in order to ascertain exact dates and times and try to get our client to give us a full description. We both knew Mogsey and what his boat looked like, he had also given us quite a lot of information already and made it clear that he couldn't say when except for overnight. "We can definitely help you but it will take time, can you borrow Ziggy's boat for now until we can find solid evidence and your boat?" I asked, he nodded, "Pose suh, Feem ting nut guh lakka di clappers doah." "Its better than nothing while we investigate all lines of enquiry." Goldie commented tussling and wielding her pencil around as she punched the air every now and again, trying to gain control over Amélie who was equally intent on getting hold of the pencil and paper.

The scene was quite unbelievable, shocking really. Poor Mogsey, he must have thought we were barking mad. If only he could see what was really happening, instead his mind was sent reeling, unable to comprehend the images he was seeing. I watched him look away, rub his eyes and then turn back to see if he really was seeing this. He was!

I snatched the pencil from Goldie's hand and in doing so managed to knock Amélie to the floor, where she stayed muttering some absurdities in French. Both Goldie and I escorted Mogsey outside, as he commented on how Iberville was looking and us promising we would keep him updated with any news but for now he should stay safe and within easy reach. He seemed happy with that, well. As we walked back into the drawing room, Goldie reminded me that we hadn't discussed any fees with him and we needed to make some money, I assured her we would all in good time.

I then addressed the elephant in the room if you pardon the pun! "What do you think you were doing, you can be so annoying?" I said irked by Amélie's carry on. "Annoyance is in the eye of the beholder, for it says far more about the one being reactive instead of responding with calmness, remember" came her reply which riled me even more. "Don't rise to it" Goldie uttered, "as for you, Amélie you silly old hag, go and haunt somewhere else for a while and LEAVE US ALONE!" Without another word or glance Amélie disappeared through the wall, leaving Goldie and I to think about the way forward.

CHAPTER 23

We climbed into Goldie's wagon and both jumped, the last thing we expected to see was Amélie sat waiting patiently on the back seat. I know shock can be good, but it can also be bad, however in this situation it is a signal that we will have to make a change in our game plan. "Amélie, what are you doing here?" I asked her as politely as I could trying not to let the irritation I was feeling come through in my voice. "I want to come with you, I want to help, it will be fun us all working together." The heartfelt sigh that escaped Goldie's lips was slow, her brain needing that time to process that we were stuck with this ghost whether we liked it or not, her eyes fixed on the back seat. "I won't get in the way, I promise, I will stay invisible, I want to help, please." Amélie said staring back at Goldie almost pleading. "You are invisible you stupid woman, you will be a hinderance to our mission, stay out of it." Goldie replied, I looked at Amélie, she looked completely dejected and for the first time I actually felt sorry for her.

I needed to defend her, "She could actually be quite useful, don't forget she specialises in unique abilities, she can get into places we can't." I said looking at Goldie as she let out a deep moan this time, "s'il vous plaît, regardez, je jure que je serai bon" the ghost replied mimicking a cross on her dress with her fingers. "Ok, ok, but you stay out of trouble, do you hear me, you are not going to wreck this opportunity for us, got it?" Goldie replied quite sternly, Amélie nodded and clapped her hands together like an excited child.

We drove to the beach as we thought it would be as good a place as any to start. From there we could gather any evidence we could find around Mogsey's boat anchorage and start collecting statements from the locals in case they had seen or heard anything.

Packing every good detective devices; ultraviolet lights, dusting powder, note books, cameras etc we started to make our way down the beach, Amélie following at snails pace behind muttering in French that we were insensitive bringing her back to place where she died five years or so ago. Goldie wanted to remind her that she had invited herself, so it was her own fault. I nudged her and whispered, "Ignore her, it's the best way." She smiled and waved at Blot who was just wading back ashore after catching bait with his net.

Blot tipped the bait into his bucket as we began to ask a few pertinent questions. Of course Blot being Blot had been in his own little world and hadn't seen or heard anything to do with Mogsey's boat, however things took a slightly unusual twist and not for the better, when he revealed that Mogsey had not turned up to buy his bait from him this morning. "Thats odd, when he left us I thought he was going to borrow Ziggy's boat for the time being?" Blot nodded, "Suh did wi he spoke tuh Ziggy bout ih wen he leff yuh an ih did all agreed Buh Ziggy's boat a still yah Luk. Nuh Mogsey.

Blot took us to Ziggy's boat, nothing had been touched, the fishing equipment was laid out ready, it didn't add up. Mogsey was the not the type of fisherman to miss a days fishing. He loved being on the water, "Those strings of light that wave upon the ocean top, come as music to my eyes, in a form of silent poetry" he would say, no idea where he learned that from. He would always fish for as long as he needed then it was back to the bar for the rest of the evening, he was a creature of habits. Sometimes he could be seen sitting on the roof of his lockup smoking a joint waiting for Blot, but not today.

We made some notes, took photos and dusted for prints, then went to where the boat was normally anchored. Some larger fragments of ropes were still tied to the buoy, some of them cut, but for the most part untied from his boat, this did not look like anyone wanting to make a quick get away. I put on some gloves and untied the rope fragments from the buoy as Goldie held open a large evidence bag. " We will need to take this for a while." I told Blot, he just nodded, poor guy, he looked completely bewildered by it all.
He strolled over to Mogsey's lock up with us, nothing, it was completely locked up. Goldie held the rusted padlock in her hand and despite her efforts attempting an illegal break-in

with a hair pin commented, "Doesn't look like this place has been opened in years, it won't budge."

Engrossed in our work, we didn't even notice that our ghostly apparition was nowhere to be seen, hopefully she had decided against staying where she had met her demise and thought of better places to haunt, let's hope wherever she was it wasn't going to be trouble and that she was all right.

Making our way to Ziggy's bar, you could hear the usual hub of activity, music blaring, loud voices having conversations. But this time Ziggy greeted us outside the bar, he seemed unusually worried. He had not seen Mogsey at all today and something was not right, it was completely out of the norm, he had got his boat ready in case Mogsey wanted to use it, but nothing. No one had seen him since he left the bar yesterday, we tried to allay Ziggy's worries by saying that he had come to us early this morning and he was well and in good spirits then, well as good as spirits go when your livelihood has been stolen. Goldie and I looked at each other, could we be looking at a missing person as well as a lost boat, it all had to be linked somehow didn't it?

I took hold of Ziggy's arm, "I'm sure he is ok, probably off smoking a joint somewhere different or looking for his boat himself, you know what he is like." Ziggy tried to smile unconvinced by my attempt to ease his concern and if I am honest, I wasn't convinced myself, I had a gnawing feeling inside that something was wrong too.

We continued our investigation inside the bar, taking statements from everyone, not a single clue emerged, nobody had seen anything untoward. I know for sure they were all telling the truth as the locals look out for one another and that is particularly true of the fishing fraternity here.

Our job to find the boat was going to be notoriously difficult. Whilst a car's numberplate is added to a searchable national database which makes it easily traceable, there is no such database for small boats, not even by their hull identification numbers. If we accept the view that Mogsey's boat is stolen, we do not have long, we will have to be decisive in our plan, as the thieves will be looking to get the boat out of sight as quickly as possible. Most boat owners have a healthy dose of 'other-boat envy,' and make mental notes of any boats they see being tampered with or removed, they are able to recognise the make and model almost instantly.

As for Mogsey, I called his mobile, it rang but remained unanswered and clicked to voicemail so I left a message asking him to contact us urgently. I went onto my apps page on my mobile in the hope he had his 'find my phone' location app switched on, but to no avail. Goldie checked on social media sites just in case he had been active on them, it can be an important indication of when he went missing.

However, it often works more effectively if you circulate a picture with as many details as possible, include any identifying marks, clothing they were last known to wear, and last-known location. Even the smallest bit of information can lead us to finding Mogsey. I called the local medical centre and police station but he had not been admitted or arrested!

Thankfully Ziggy had a tatty photo stuck to a piece of wood at the back of the bar, he removed it and handed it to us. Despite its state, you could clearly see Mogsey and his boat, at least it might help jog peoples memories as we show it around, and upload to the web, someone must know or have seen something surely? If anyone posts a comment we can follow it up straight away, any information could be valuable.

We also thought about taking it to the Alise and asking Pia to post for us. We were after all concerned about the safety and well-being of Mogsey and telling our story and sharing photos and information might help. Typically the paper will give viewers a tip line or direct phone number to reach out to if they have additional information regarding the search, but we had already posted on social media so that would do the same job for now.

Just as Goldie and I were about to leave the bar, a fisherman walked in, "Dees man dem a a luk fah Mogsey an fi im boat any ideas." Ziggy asked quick off the mark and slamming a glass of rum down in from of him. He looked us up and down, "Haven't seen him, is he missing? Was the boat fitted with a GPS tracker?" Ok so we really need to find Mogsey this was not right, he wasn't away for long even if he did decide to wander. On the boat front, that was something Goldie and I hadn't even considered, our boat knowledge was pretty thin. Mmhm, having said that there's no guarantee that fitting a GPS tracker to the boat would actually help us to pinpoint its location. If it was a professional job rather than an opportunistic one, the thieves will have done their homework, traced the wiring to search for a hidden tracker and ripped it out, the fastest way possible.

We left the bar to trawl the neighbouring streets looking for Mogsey and any boats covered and uncovered, parked behind abandoned buildings, or on any dishevelled green space. We passed around the photo of Mogsey and checked all the dilapidated buildings in the hope we might find him holed up there.

CHAPTER 24

We spent most of the day drawing blanks at every turn, and felt quite frustrated at our lack of progress. The one thing that was going to keep our spark alive in this was the necessity to find Mogsey as soon as possible. As we drove off we started to discuss if we had missed any avenues, neither of us could come up with any plausible explanations as to what was going on. A sudden aroma of sweet peach filled the air before Amélie unexpectedly appeared on the back seat of the truck, scaring the living daylights out of both of us. "Guess what? I have found something of great interest to you both" she uttered in her French accent, completely unaware of the effect her sudden entrance had had on us. One minute the road ahead was there, wide open and safe, the next, came loud screeching noises as Goldie struggled with the truck to stop it veering up a grass verge and smashing into the derelict cafe on the approaching corner.

Once she had expertly regained control and brought the car to a halt, we looked at one another in a newfound silence and both caught our breath, before turning to face Amélie. "Yuh foofool duppy Yuh cudda get wi kill Wah mek nuh yuh jus guh an drop out" Goldie yelled, her anger at this moment in time building like steam in a pressure cooker, she needed to find a way to let it out in a safe manner before she committed the gruesome murder of a ghost, if that is possible. Amélie shouted back, "Vous vous disputez pour rien, pour ne rien gagner et c'est à mes dépens. C'est stressant et blessant pour moi. Vous êtes soulagé, je suis stressé, qu'est-ce que je suis censé faire avec ça?" Well, that was like fuelling the fire which now evolved into a high pitched episode of French and Jamaican screeching dialects, neither of them with any clue as to what each other was saying. "Stop it, stop it, right now, it isn't helping." I bellowed at an appropriate moment in order to be heard, my timing seemed to work, there was silence. I cleared my throat, "Lets all just calm down shall we, Amélie that was really irresponsible, you could have trashed Goldie's truck and got us killed, don't ever do that again, do you understand?" Amélie nodded, as I turned to face Goldie, "I know she is an irritant and totally annoying but she is just a ghost, don't rise to her stupid antics."

Amélie sat back in the seat pouting and folding her arms, whilst Goldie turned to face the road once more, her eyes narrowing as her hands gripped the steering wheel. Phew, now what? We were at a stalemate.

Suddenly Amélie broke the silence. "All right then, I am very sorry, I didn't want to harm you, I was just excited to tell you what I have found that was all, please don't be cross with me." "Thank you Amélie, apology accepted," I replied nudging Goldie, who eventually let out an exasperated sigh,

"Yes, yes, sorry for shouting and all that," she replied clenching her jaw, as she turned to face Amélie still antagonised by the situation. "Tell us what you have found that's so important," I asked trying to keep the situation calm and under control. "Mogsey is still at the beach, I think." She replied grinning and clapping her hands together, quite pleased with her findings.

It felt as if Goldie was a smouldering volcano, ready to erupt again at any opportunity, "Is that it, is that all you have, you stupid ghost, you, you appear here, nearly ruin my truck and try to kill us in the process, just to tell us that!" Amélie looked like she was about to burst into tears at any moment. I felt sorry for her for the second time in the same day, she had succumbed to a rough life, her home life had been turmoil and violent, not constantly, but enough to make her less stable than she could have been.

I poked Goldie to stop "what?" She shouted. "Lets just hear the rest of it before jumping to conclusions, shall we?" I said looking at Amélie, "Ok, how do you know that? We have already searched the beach and surrounding area and found nothing." "Well, I have seen him, I think" came her answer. I looked at Goldie confused and bewildered, "You think you saw him?" Amélie nodded and crossed her heart with her hands. "We need to go back to the beach," I had an uneasy feeling that Amélie was telling the truth and I was almost sure Mogsey was not going to be in good shape."Of course we do Jaz, because the ghost has a hunch." Goldie replied, rolling her eyes. Amélie opened her mouth ready to reply as I shook my head to silence her, "Ghost be silent, not another word" Goldie uttered as she restarted the engine.

At this point I must say that the relationship between Goldie and Amélie was becoming more like an alliance of convenience, if they have to work together, they will put up with one another. Amélie's emotions were alien to her, she had barely understood her own feelings when she was alive, let alone anyone else's, I have to admit though she was a bit like a bad penny, always showing up at the most inappropriate times.

We arrived back at the beach in record time and climbed out of the car. "Are you coming then, Amélie?" I asked. She hesitated before getting out of the car. "je te préviens c'est pas sympa." She sniffed, "What?" Goldie looked at me hoping for some sort of enlightenment. "Not nice was what she said." We stood momentarily before Goldie snapped, clearly still irritated by the ghosts antics. "What is she on about, Ok where now?" Her refusal to smile or show any warmth at all was her subtle form of emotional warfare, it was hardly fair, after all our ghost was only trying to be helpful.

Amélie floated across the beach to Mogsey's store and disappeared, leaving us wondering where she had gone and what on earth our next move was. "Foofool duppy Anedda wild goose chase Wah a shi playing…." Before Goldie could finish the sentence Amélie reappeared, "Shh, she may be onto something, remember she can see things and get into places we can't." I said. "You really don't want to go in there," she said with what resembled a grimace and pointing at the corrugated store. Goldie and I looked at one another, baffled as to how we could get inside, just as Blot arrived with his bucket of bait. I had never noticed his aroma before, the smell, if you could enjoy the fishiness as a great recipe in the air that told so many fishy stories. "Any news?" he asked.

Amélie sat herself down on the sand, if anyone could sit in a manner that transmits a sense of grace and intelligent poise, then she had mastered it. She sniffed and held her hand over her nose, "Cette puanteur piquante me fait catapulter quand je suis mort." She uttered, "What are you on about now?" Goldie replied in a contentious manner, luckily Amélie decided not rise to the occasion, as I roughly translated, " Something about pungent stench and death." Goldie raised her eyebrows and rolled her eyes. "Are you two ok? You seem a bit nervous, like you have seen a ghost. Blot commented.

If only he knew, instead it was a polite way of telling us were demented, it was easy to forget that only we could see the ghost! "Yes, sorry, we wanted to take a look inside, we think it might help with our investigation, but the door is still firmly secured by the padlock." I replied as Goldie tried once more unsuccessfully to pick the lock. "Its far to rusted" she said.

Blot placed his bucket down almost on top of Amélie, but she had the quick thinking to roll out of the way, we giggled. "Oh he neva guh eena dat way he eva deh removes one addi corrugated panels at di bac." Blot replied. Now that was a turn up for the books, we were completely dumbfounded, we had never anticipated this for a moment, there was much more to this investigating lark! "And you failed to tell us that the first time because?" I asked Blot, he sensed the annoyance in my voice. "Hush Mi jus figet Hab mi hampered di investigation?" "Yes," Goldie snapped again as we all walked round to the back of the store where Blot proceeded to point out the loose panel.

I could kick myself for missing this when we investigated before but it wasn't obvious to anyone that the panel was removable. "Need anything else from me or can I go and sell my bait?" Blot asked picking up his bucket and managing to bump it into Amélie. "Regarde ce que tu fais, espèce d'homme stupide." She uttered waggling a boney finger at him and standing up, brushing sand off of her dress. "No thats fine, we can take it from here" we replied together.

Funny how everyone seemed to be able to speak English at this moment in time, normally I have to try and work out the conversation myself from the odd words I do understand!

We removed the panel and crawled inside, Amélie had already morphed herself inside and was staring at the floor in the corner. That's when we noticed him. If you've never seen the transition from human to corpse, the moment the soul passes on, I can tell you, it is always a very moving experience, every fond memory you have sparks up, as if the soul is trying to make an SOS for the person to return. Seeing Mogsey dead, his cadaver, his body without life, he looked so different, making the situation real in ways that are hard to transmit.

CHAPTER 25

Mogsey was lying in the half-light, utterly still, eyes open as if admiring the heavens, his ivory skin splattered and his face half submerged in the gritty sand, any cursory glance is enough to know he has been dead a while. I knelt beside him, his lips were already blue, skin grey, eyes dull with exploded pupils. Goldie managed to rip away another panel, luckily they were only corrugated iron so it wasn't too difficult.

Now we could see more, he looked grotesque, his eyes were swollen and congealed bloody spit drooled from his slack jaw, there were great purple welts over his skin where his clothes had been ripped. Most importantly and the probable cause of his demise was his throat, which had been slit straight across with either a straight razor or knife. He would have staggered backwards before he fell as some of the panels were sprayed crimson with his blood. On closer inspection his carotid arteries had been severed, which means he would have passed out after a few seconds due to lack of oxygenated blood to the brain, he would have literally drowned in his own blood, an almost instantaneous death, which I suppose was the one saving grace.

My nostrils filled with the smell of blood and my stomach lurched, all of this bloodshed was as barbaric as it was stupid, it was evil and cruel. What had Mogsey ever done to deserve this? I stood up and glanced at Goldie who was looking for more clues amongst the debris strewn around. The sand was the perfect consistency to hold the shape of any imprint, but no, the killer hadn't left their shoe impression here, or any clues we could see, they were very careful.

Goldie dug into her pocket for a sticky sweet only to find the sweet wrapper was empty, her face fell a little, not a good omen for a new case. But then her fingers grasped onto one that had fallen out the wrapper, she pulled it out and held it up to the light, there was minimal pocket fluff, so she popped it into her mouth, "It helps me to think." She commented as she continued. "There are obvious signs of a struggle, Mogsey certainly put up a fight before he met his killer, thats for sure." She uttered, I have to agree with her there. "Yes, and it has to be someone who knows what they were doing, it takes a certain amount of expertise to land such a strike with a knife or blade and from the force inflicted, it has to be a man who committed the act."

Amélie bent over Mogsey and opened his clasped hand "What are you doing?" I asked her, "Look he has my locket" came her reply, "What!" Goldie and I both said together, as we inspected a bit more closely. She repeated herself, "He has my locket." She removed it and put it around her neck. "You can't do that," I told her, "why not?" "It is evidence from a crime scene and the locket just looks weird hung in mid air, remember it is only us that unfortunately can see you!" Goldie uttered as Amélie tutted and pulled a face but kept the locket securely hung around her neck. "We really need to call this in to the authorities, this is not a missing person or kidnapping anymore, it's a murder investigation, any signs of the murder weapon yet?" I said to Goldie. She nodded and shook her head, before saying, "Ok but only to my uncle and his colleagues, then we can continue this as our investigation. It will be good to have our first case as a murder, and no, I haven't found the murder weapon yet."

Seems like a fair deal, we may need some help as we are still new to this and her uncle did say he would be there for us if we needed him. We still had a lot of unanswered questions that need solutions, also I keep getting the image of Tilly drowning in my mind, could this be a clue. Amélie must have read my thoughts, I hate it when she does that! "Tilly," she uttered, "I have told you before she is back and not dead but you won't believe me." Goldie finished taking some photographs and dusted for fingerprints before removing her gloves, "Nothing," she tutted, this just doesn't make any sense, we watched her drown but maybe Amélie, as much as it pains me to admit it, may have a point."

I carried on searching behind some covered bait buckets, allowing the light to illuminate boxes, lots of brown boxes.

Could Mogsey be caught up in some sort of smuggling operation. I put on gloves and with my penknife sliced right through the brown card. Inside were large bottles of Perrier water, no different in styling to the kind we buy from the local mart. I removed one glove and tipped a little of the "water" onto my hand. It seemed to evaporate quickly and had a familiar coolness to it, possibly alcohol? Likely close to one hundred percent proof. After Goldie had insisted on a sniff I replaced the cap and placed it back in the box, we really did need Goldie's uncle.

I turned around only to find Goldie and Amélie in yet another altercation. Amélie had opened and drunk the entire contents of one of the bottles and was now acting quite goofily, tumbling when she tried to walk, her eyes lagging when she looked in a new direction, speech slurring slightly as Goldie tried to remove the bottle from her vice like grip. Thats when it hit me. "Wait a moment, I think I have it, well, sort of." Goldie shivered then stood motionless as Amélie wobbled through her and remained propped up beside her. "Don't do that." Goldie said to Amélie, this time there was no heat, just a sense of sheer exasperation in her voice. "I am still not convinced it is Tilly but whoever it is, got into Iberville, stole the locket and killed Mogsey as a way to get to us, they knew we would try and seek them out." I said. Amélie was like some quizzical nodding dog as Goldie and I bounced ideas off one another.

"Ok Jaz, so say that is right, why did whoever it was pick Mogsey, and why do they need to get to us, if your assumption is correct, then the only person it has to be is Tilly, wanting revenge. She knows we know Mogsey and would want to track down his killer. Perhaps she didn't drown, she just made us think she did, she is after all devious on all levels." Mmhm good point. "Ok it still doesn't add up though, why has Mogsey got all these bottles full of alcohol, maybe the two are completely unrelated and he was killed as part of a smuggling ring?" I uttered. Goldie picked a piece of sweet out of her tooth, "never thought he would be involved in anything like this, the other angle is that option one with Tilly involved and then Mogsey was framed, this stuff put here." Yes, that was certainly another avenue to explore.

Whilst I continued to explore the lock up, Goldie phoned her uncle and briefly explained the situation we had unearthed. He was amazed that we had become embroiled in something so grim on our first case and would get to us straight away.

CHAPTER 26

Goldie's uncle, the Commissioner, arrived quickly in an unmarked car along with two of his police colleagues and a black mortuary van, very organised. He surveyed the scene and looked over Mogsey's body, "We need to get Mogsey out of here swiftly and cordon off the crime scene before the locals get wind of this, otherwise we will be stuck here for hours and local gossip will make things worse than they already are" he commented to the two officers as he walked around the lock up.

The calm nature of the police officers was a welcoming vibe, they both had broad smiles and offered up kind words, one of them beckoned to the mortuary man, who duly obeyed and stepped forward. Since taking over the complete organisation of police on the Island, Goldie's uncle has worked wonders. He says that we need to know that when we call the police, they will come and help. If they are trained and supported properly, the entire community will be reassured by their presence and that was definitely true for us today.

As they helped put Mogsey into the van and seal off the crime scene we continued to explain to Goldie's uncle what had led us to the current situation. After listening intently, he agreed to us continuing with this as our case, we were after all legally registered as detectives now. We discussed our current theories and possible ways forward, the commissioner felt it was the correct plan of attack for now but warned us that we would need to be adaptable as the situation may change, we also needed to search for the murder weapon.

Suddenly out of the corner of my eye I caught sight of Amélie just about to disappear through one of the panels, no doubt to annoy the police officers outside. I lurched forward and managed to grab hold of the locket, ripping it from her neck. She screamed and put her hands to her neck, I didn't think ghosts felt anything! "tu .... rends ça, c'est à moi, regarde tu m'as fait saigner." She uttered, "now's not the time and you are not bleeding!" Goldie sniggered. "Everything all right?" The Commissioner asked. Goldie and I glanced at one another, we needed to cover this debacle quickly, "Yes, sorry, for that, I was just thinking out loud, this locket was stolen from my home and ended up here." I held out my hand to show him as I finished the sentence, luckily for us he only saw the locket in my hand and not as it was floating in mid air a moment before. He replied, "Seriously, I think this is a set up and Mogsey has been framed, I would never in a million years take him as a thief or pirate smuggling illegal contraband. A pain in the preverbal, a jack the lad, sometimes a drunk but for all his character flaws he was a lovable rogue and had a heart of gold." "Yes, agreed unc, we don't think Mogsey stole it either, we are definitely working on the assumption that he was framed, possibly to get to Jaz and I, for what happened with Ed Wrexham and Tilly, it all has to be linked, we just need to fathom out how."

The commissioner mopped his forehead, "I think we all need to look at this freshly in the morning, for now let's put the panels back and go home, I have a function I need to attend. I will meet you both back here tomorrow, see if anything new comes to light overnight, say about ten, is that suitable?" We both nodded in agreement and shook his hand before heading outside.

We replaced the panels and turned to go, only to see the two officers stood next to one another looking very puzzled as their hats seemed to fall onto the sand, as soon as they picked them up and placed them on their heads, off they would fall again. They looked to the sky and one of them licked their finger, holding in the air to see if wind was the cause. Sadly no, this wave of insanity was Amélie, taking great joy in knocking the hats off of their heads and dancing around them clapping like some small child having the time of its life.

If there is any chance of us trying to solve the madness of the world, we need to start by getting our ghost under control. As the policemen walked back to the car, Amélie started to chase after them, until Goldie managed to grab her by the ear and haul her backwards. "Stay here, you looney apparition" she uttered. Amélie brushed her hand away, "I am not a lunatic or an apparition," I am creative and free spirited." Mmhm right!

Ghost in tow, we went back to the truck, climbed inside and made our way back to Iberville. It had been such a full-on day, we hadn't even stopped for lunch and were now starving. "Can I have my locket back now?" Amélie asked leaning forward in the back seat. "No" we both said together. She sat back again, arms folded and never uttered another word for the rest of the short journey.

We reached Iberville and made ourselves something to eat, Goldie had agreed to stay the night in my partly demolished house. "Can I have some food please, I am slightly peckish too" Amélie asked politely sitting down at the kitchen table, "I beg your pardon, ghosts don't need to eat," I replied. "Surprise! Looks like this one thinks she can," Goldie commented, nodding in Amélie's direction as we watched her trying to help herself to some pasta and ram it down her throat as quickly as she could, "pas mal" she uttered before disappearing into the ether, "I'll give her not bad, she is lucky to have some." I replied.

CHAPTER 27

We awoke the next morning to the sound of workmen whistling, banging and clanking. We must have been exhausted and had literally fallen asleep at the kitchen table. Somehow bits of last nights food debris was stuck to us, even a half filled bottle of wine stared back, screaming drink me, drink me. Goldie rose from her chair and straightened herself awkwardly, I too felt quite stiff, she made breakfast before we got ourselves sorted in time to meet the Commissioner, we couldn't be late.

Goldie was well known for her homemade breakfasts although I have to say I was not really that keen right now, but we needed something to keep us going for the day in more ways than one that was for sure! I watched her as she concentrated on spreading the avocado, not too thinly over four pieces of toast and sprinkled tomato and some green stuff on top as if it were cake decorations. There was a sort of joy in how she did it, as if she was happily absorbed by a feeling of love that played in her subtle smile and soft gaze. Eventually she brought it over to the table along with some very strong coffee, which helped take the food taste away.

Before we left, I made sure the builders knew their plans and were on track, letting them know to reach me on my mobile if needed. So far our ghostly nightmare had not surfaced this morning, hopefully she had lost interest and found someone else to haunt or something along those lines. We decided as we were early to visit the morgue on the way to Mogsey's lock up, to see if there were any further developments that could help us.

As we walked inside the morgue, we were met by the same petite bronzed lady who had led me down the same sterile corridor to the metal door when I came to visit Winston and Candice a few years back. I shivered, it was freezing cold in here, a complete contrast to the warm sun outside. This time she introduced herself as Lucile but showed no signs of recognising me from any previous encounters.

Inside the examination room it was eerily quiet except for the buzz of the fluorescent lights that beamed brightly as if to counter the gloom in the room, the hum of the dictaphone, as its tape spins round on the counter and the air conditioning whirling softly as if in silent mourning for the dead. The floor was solid concrete, rough and very cold underfoot, even with shoes on, it felt like you could get frostbite if you stood still too long. The walls were painted a ghostly dark grey and the ceiling was high but still loomed, giving an intimidating feeling.

Everything in this room reminded us of the cruelty and power death brings and reminds us of how sacred living is, we need to appreciate it all the more. We introduced ourselves to the morgue attendant called Hector Lex, an odd, sad man. Despite the pristine white overall he wore, it was very evident from his haunted eyes, wrinkled face and pursed lips that he had witnessed a lot of death and mourning in this room which had taken its toll on his outlook in his own life.

A cold sweat began to break out over my hands and forehead coupled with a nauseous feeling, I retreated and stood behind Goldie as she continued to whisper to Hector Lex and shuffled her feet awkwardly fearing she would wake the sleeping dead.

Mogsey lay on a stainless steel table, naked under a white sheet, his toes poking out to reveal attached toe tags. Hector Lex pulled back the sheet slightly to Mogsey's waistline. His skin was badly bruised bold and bright, spreading purple with yellow blotches across his skin surface. His slashed throat had been expertly stitched up and was now a dry brown wound. "Interesting case this," Hector Lex uttered softly lifting up one of Mogsey's arms and reaching for a pair of small forceps, as he continued. I removed my notebook ready to start scribbling, my confidence returning once more, this wasn't so bad and I felt intrigued. "So ladies, on closer examination, there is contamination under the nails. If you look here you can see tiny fibres of blue cotton cloth, do you see?" Goldie and I peered closely, but shook our heads, we could see nothin

Hector Lex pulled down a large magnifying glass from a ceiling pendant I hadn't noticed before and pointed to underneath Mogsey's index finger with his tweezers. Sure enough there were tiny fragments of blue, how he managed to come to the conclusion it was blue cotton, god only knows. He continued, "The other two things to note are that his cause of death was not by having his throat cut, as you would imagine, that came after. Instead in this particular case, he died from asphyxiation, strangulation."

Goldie and I looked at each other in complete astonishment as Hector Lex said, "Look at the bruising and fingernail scratches on his neck and these small reddish, purple splotches in his eyes." Goldie and I looked, as Hector held open Mogsey's eye lids for us to observe. He then held up an X-ray and pointed out a fracture of the U-shaped hyoid bone at the base of Mogsey's tongue. "I took a sample from his lungs and found some evidence of foam." Goldie and I were confused. "Asphyxiation can sometimes produce foam in the airways as the victim struggles to breathe, the mucus from the lungs mixes with air, hence causing foaming." Hector Lex revealed. "And the second thing of note?" I asked. "Now this is where it gets very interesting indeed." Hector Lex answered.

Goldie and I moved forward slightly, bending over Mogsey's torso,"Do you see the congealed brownish blood spit on the side of Mogsey's mouth?" He asked. We both nodded before replying "yes." Hector Lex removed a small cylindrical looking object from its case, flicked the switch to reveal an ultra violet light which he waved over the side of the mouth. "Do you see?" We both peered closer, our need to know and see more taking a precedent over the aroma a dead body gives off.

We both looked at each other, "A fingerprint," we said in unison. "Exactly a fingerprint of sorts and a woman's at that, obviously she tried to wipe away some of the blood from his mouth in a small guilt ridden attempt to clean him up a bit." Hector Lex said switching off the purple light. "How can you tell the fingerprint belongs to a woman?" Goldie questioned. "Woman exhibit higher RD than males." "What does that mean in simple terms?" I asked "Put simply it means women have narrower ridges on their fingers compared to males." Hector Lex replied.

This has been really helpful, it was a good move for us to swing past the morgue on our way to meet the Commissioner. The Commissioner, oh no, Goldie's phone buzzed with a text from her uncle asking if we were thinking of joining him at any point today. We told Hector Lex that we needed to go but would be in contact again, he was more than pleased to be of any assistance he could to help our case.

As we turned to leave I looked back, "Hector Lex, is there anyway of lifting that fingerprint and running it through the database for us?" I asked, Goldie winked, "Good thinking Jaz!" "Already one step ahead my friends," he replied, "but there is a problem. Fingerprints have four main patterns, called arches, loops, ridges and whorls. The shape, size, number and arrangement of any minor details in these patterns are what make each fingerprint unique.

On this occasion, this woman has somehow destroyed her basal layer, which means, the fingerprint has narrow ridges, so you can tell it belongs to a woman, but as the other three are missing, it draws a blank on all databases." Great just when we thought we were getting somewhere. "Oh, how could she destroy her basal layer thing?" I asked. "Well, could be through plastic surgery, a bad cut that has needed stitches or a burn, anything like that, but it means you can't even get a close match." Hector Lex answered, ushering us out of the room as Goldie's phoned buzzed again, a growing inpatient Commissioner on the other end!

CHAPTER 28

As we arrived at Mogsey's lock up, we were greeted with sight that was a clue that the day was only going to get worse.

The Commissioner was sat on a chair placed strategically on the sand next to the lock up, reading a newspaper. His two policemen were standing either side of him like centuries ready to protect against any force of nature that came their way. Goldie giggled and nudged me, there was no real need, I got the joke immediately, the Commissioner looked like he was Captain James T. Kirk, Commander of the Starship Enterprise! What we didn't expect was to see Amélie playing hopscotch in front of them, a reminder of childhood games we used to play.

The sun was beating down and yet for our eyes only she was in a jumper and some tweed trousers hopping madly amid shells and markers she had drawn with a piece of wood. It took a second or two for the image to sink it, despite it being right before our eyes, larger than life. I felt my lips stretch wider into gaping grin and my eyebrows arch for the sky, if you think about it, this world is quite astonishing, full of some sort of dysfunction at every turn.

Once she had caught our gaze she skipped over to Goldie and me, throwing her arms around our necks but in truth missing completely. "Bonjour, mon amis, j'attends depuis un moment. Quel est notre plan pour aujourd'hui?" "You stupid.." "Goldie, hush" I said stopping her mid sentence, I didn't want another day of constant sniping between the two of them. "I won't be a nuisance, I promise I really want to help." Goldie shook her head and moved towards the Commissioner, waving as she went. "Sorry Unc, we got waylaid." He uttered no words, just smiled and looked at his watch as he rose from his chair and went inside the lock up, with us in tow.

Once inside we told him everything we had discovered at the morgue. "Mmhm intriguing" was all he said initially, before following it up with "do you have any idea of who the perpetrator is? "Jaz has a theory but nothing circumstantial yet, we need more evidence. It does look more like it could be Tilly but we have nothing concrete to say it was her or to place her at the scene of the crime" Goldie answered, "Just a hunch really." I added. "I see, sometimes instincts are right" the Commissioner replied as we continued to examine the crime scene trying to gather more forensic evidence that could ultimately lead to the detection and prosecution of whoever committed this evil act. To follow through on our hunch, we also needed proof that Tilly was actually alive.

We took some more photos, searched for the murder weapon, and signs of any footprints or marks indicating that items in the shed may have been moved. I collected some swab samples from the blood splattered on the panels and looked for further fibres of clothes that may be of help to Hector Lex.

The policemen then loaded all the boxes of contraband into the police truck whilst the Commissioner looked on, giving orders. Both Goldie and I had the added job of staying on top of trying to keep our friendly irritant, Amélie, out of the way. As she had mastered the art of moving things, she started some investigative work of her own. I am sure Goldie's uncle was aware of the strange goings on, but seemed to take all the madness around him in his stride, he was so laid back. Only once did we see him raise his eyebrows as he grabbed hold of a fishing rod and net that appeared to be making its way across the lock up of its own accord!

The rest of our morning we were occupied with work to secure the crime scene, documenting, investigating and evidencing clues that could put a time to the murder or that might help us explain the events in order to help piece together a possible scenario. By lunchtime, we had done all we could. The one major disappointment was that we still had not found any murder weapon, there was nothing here that could have been used to strangle Mogsey and there was certainly no evidence of a knife or blade, only fishing lines but that couldn't be strong enough to cut Mogsey's throat, could it? "Goldie, Commissioner, I think we are deliberately being thrown off course." I uttered. "What do you mean Jaz?"

they both replied together. "Well, we have been looking for a knife or blade haven't we?" They both nodded, "And we know from Hector Lex that Mogsey was strangled first, before his throat was cut." "What are you getting at?" Goldie asked. "What if it wasn't a knife or blade at all, what if Mogsey was strangled with a fishing line. It can be deadly, easily concealable or disposable. It could have easily cut into his neck and sliced through his carotid arteries at the same time strangulation occurred, maybe the perpetrator didn't anticipate the fishing line on slicing Mogsey's neck open, maybe they just wanted to strangle him." "Yes, yes, that is a very plausible option, but either way it would still lead to death. We need to start looking for fishing line with traces of blood on it, if it hasn't been wiped clean already." Goldie replied her excitement bubbling over.

Goldie's uncle looked amazed at our deduction." I knew Locked and Loaded would be a good duo, I have taught you both well, please continue your search, I need to address the noise outside. Don't let me stop your investigation" he uttered walking towards the opening in the lock up. We had been so engrossed in our investigation we were unaware of any noise.

We followed him outside, only to be nosey you understand. A large crowd of locals had now gathered and the two policemen were having a hard time trying to keep them under control. The crowd seemed to have a life of its own, their vibrant clothes all shining in the sun, everyone moving as if unseen hands were dragging them this way and that, pulling their eyes to one thing and then another. I had never felt claustrophobic before, but in this almighty swell of angry humanity I felt fear rise in my chest. As they surged forward shouting at the Commissioner, Goldie and I moved backwards almost as if there was risk to our life.

The Commissioner straightened his uniform then clapped, the air fell silent as he began to address them. "My friends, by now you will have all heard rumours that Mogsey has been killed. Unfortunately the rumours are true, he was an unfortunate victim of a targeted crime and has lost his life as a consequence. What I should like is for you all to go back to your daily routines and not hamper our ongoing investigation that is expertly being carried out with the assistance of private investigators, Locked and Loaded." That did sound funny. "Meanwhile I would like to encourage you to come forward if you have any information or sightings that could aid the investigation. We will release more information as we know more, none of you are in danger, I must stress this was a targeted attack, now please disperse from the crime scene and let us get on with finding Mogsey's killer quickly, thank you."

The gathered crowd obeyed, gradually dispersing and making their way off the beach and back to their daily chores. I felt quite humbled that they could all have the same feelings at the same time, so much kinship and camaraderie, you can never be lonely in the Caribbean.

CHAPTER 29

Over the next few days and nights Goldie and I kept ourselves busy trying to solve Mogsey's murder, trouble was every avenue we explored seemed to come up with less and less clues, this was a very good cover up indeed, maybe a professional who knew exactly what they were doing and how to cover their tracks at every turn. I have to say it was looking more and more likely that a clone of Tilly was the culprit. We drew a blank at every corner looking for the boat as well.

However, what did come to light was that Mogsey was actually involved in the prohibited trafficking of alcohol as part of a smuggling ring. He was the person who stored the merchandise until it needed to be exported or moved then he would courier it to wherever he was told. He had been recruited through one of the organised crime networks that exploit new opportunities for their own gain. The profits from this alcohol smuggling were then used to fund other criminal activities.

We had found out about this from the National Crime Agency and their database whilst searching for Tilly and her band of 'merry men' Poor Mogsey, I know he was a character but I bet he was not made fully aware of what he had got himself involved with. When we investigated further, it transpired that Mogsey's brother had been threatened with his life after also becoming involved with a local drug cartel and had tried to escape. Mogsey was the hero so to speak, becoming embroiled in order to save his brothers life. Goldie and I never even knew he had family, unfortunately Mogsey's brother lost his life a few years ago during some contraband bust and then Mogsey was stuck fearing for his own life. Such a shame that he never told anyone, we could have helped, instead he would have just been given scanty information and promised good money for transporting and storing products. To him, this was just a little harmless dishonesty and a boost to his meagre income from fishing.

The commissioner was just as surprised when we visited his office to update him with the case. "You think you know someone and then bam" was his only comment.

Iberville became a complete building site, although you could now actually glean from the mess our visions for its future, so I spent more time at the shack with Goldie. Their plans had been put on hold until Leroy returned from his mission, it was nice staying in the shack again and it also meant that Amélie went missing, so great, we had peace and quiet and could get on with our case rather than babysit a ghost!

Goldie managed to speak with Leroy who was able to answer a couple of questions to point us towards finding solutions in our investigation. Luckily I was able to get some assistance from Tim during our few conversations, although to be fair, they mostly evolved around Iberville's progress and the costings on setting up the new distillery. Always be one step ahead in business he tells me, keep an eye on them!

Tim and I also spoke about how their mission was going. He remained hopeful that there could be a solution but there had been a recent blow to their plans, when the Maduro regime had managed to scoop up most of the state governorships vote and tried to arrange for a government-controlled court to cancel the rest of the opposition wins. Guaidó, the interim president, had made some costly mistakes which Tim couldn't divulge, which meant the only valid reason for continuing to recognise Guaidó and his team was to try to prevent valuable Venezuelan assets in America and England from falling into the hands of the Maduro regime as that would be disastrous.

I didn't really understand it all for the most part and it was made worse by me not being able to ask questions and Tim being unable to offer up too much information. I told Tim how our case was going, he gave me some pointers we hadn't thought of which was quite useful. Leroy had already told Goldie that some boats were fitted with a second GPS tracker and if that was the case we should still be able to get a real time location on Mogsey's boat. It was probably still being used to import and export illegal goods even though he had been disposed of.

I asked Tim about Tilly and finger-printing or lack of it. Tim told me that sometimes if skin is cut or burned, its tissues can grow and renew itself, shedding old cells that will possibly distort fingerprints. A recent research programme proved that prints can still be lifted from any area of skin on the hand, but only if detectives have lots of patience. If our murderer had put their hand on something we could lift and trace from there. Listening to him it all got quite complicated about how they did it, but there were different databases which stored prints. Ok that was good, Goldie and I weren't aware that there was more than one database.

The other option, as lovely as it sounds, Goldie and I would not be trying. It included lots of steps, the use of baby oil and an iodine/silver transfer method, whatever that is. Then applying heat and an iodine fuming gun was involved to direct fumes onto the victims skin, laying over a thin sheet of silver, removing the silver plate and finally, exposing the plate to a strong light, a bit like developing a photograph. Then hey presto, you can trace any finger prints.

Anyhow, several days later we were still no closer to a solution with either the murder weapon, the murderer or where Mogsey's boat was so we decided to treat ourselves to an afternoon of relaxation and recharge our batteries. We had completed lots of online searches, trawled through databases until our eyes became blurred, been back to the scene several times, revisited the morgue and carried out more local door to door investigations. Mogsey's case file was so thick it didn't shut, but why couldn't we find any answers?

CHAPTER 30

We sat on the deck of the shack, reminiscing, talking about Goldie and Leroy's plans and generally having a break from the case when we were startled by a huffing and clacking noise as this creature from the black lagoon lumbered towards the deck. Our eyes were trained on this spectacle, our heavy eyelids a fraction too slow to blink, our irises too stationary. It was as if our brains were suffering from a massive short circuit and were struggling to compute.

I wanted to say to say something, I could definitely hear the sentences in my head, all the words crawling around, moving through the maze in my mind. But they seemed to hit barriers and walls that stopped them from coming together. I looked at Goldie who was also in the same predicament as me. This sea creature was now trying awkwardly to clamber over the wooden railings of the deck, knowing they could fall onto the sand below at anytime. Its arms wanted to haul the rest of it up quickly but its muscles were not strong enough, the huffing and puffing continued as its legs tried to meet the hands and follow over the railings.

Part of me wanted to help with this struggle, I really did, but the adrenaline surging inside me, told me to stay rooted to the spot and let this thing fail, it would give us more time to escape if we needed to. Then the silence was broken. "I wish my body was wired differently, I wish I could get increased strength, its a long way down. How could I have thought this would ever be fun?" "Amélie?" We both uttered together, leaning forward for closer inspection. "Bien sûr, qui attendiez-vous?" came her reply. "Well, we were not expecting the return of an irritating ghost covered in goodness knows what that's for sure, thought we had seen the back of you" Goldie answered without hesitating. "Well, if that's all the thanks I get for all the undercover surveillance I have carried out for you and the information I have, I am off." Amélie scoffed at Goldie's comment. "Here we go again, like the information from the beach lock up I suppose." Goldie continued. "Well, I found Mogsey dead for you, didn't I?" came Amélie's reply.

This childish bickering went on back and forth like a game of verbal tennis. "ENOUGH." I shouted at both of them, hauling Amélie the rest of the way over the rail and onto the deck, removing the kelp forest stuck to her body, she looked and smelt like a large piece of plankton! The truce continued as Amélie wrung out the water from her clothes and sat down on the deck. "Amélie, before we go any further, why are you covered in seaweed and wet and why didn't you just morph yourself in front of us instead of all that performance coming over the decking rail like that?"

Amélie sighed and sprawled out like a starfish, "I need to dry off, I had to swim to find the boat and for some reason seaweed likes to stick to me, at one point I did have some small fish attached to me too, but I managed to shake them off, oh and I didn't want to scare you." "Can't you just walk on water, like a normal ghost?" Goldie sniped. Amélie sighed again before uttering, "Sometimes you need to mix things up a bit you stupide sorcière." "I said enough you two," this was tedious, why do I have to be a stress buffer for these two?

This was supposed to be a quiet relaxing time, nothing but the trees, sea and good company, where we can put our small world in order. A chance for the spinning top of ideas, that carousel of duties to slow and maybe even stop, but obviously it was an insane notion that we could relax. As Amélie remained sprawled across the deck, I asked. "Amélie, would you like to tell us what your surveillance has uncovered?" She replied with a single word, "Non." Goldie started, "You ridiculous excuse for a ghost, why can't you just tell us and make this easy?" I rolled my eyebrows glancing at a very exasperated friend, I did share her views and feelings but needed to be patient in order to get the ghost to talk.

Amélie sat up, "I am so tired." "For goodness sake, Amélie, please, just tell us what you have found out." I could feel the words begin to sound quite stern as they came out of my mouth. "I am not saying anything further until I have had time for a rest and recharge my batteries," she apologises pointing at Goldie. I nudged Goldie we needed to get this over and done with. "Ok, ok, Amélie, I am very sorry for the way I spoke to you, shall I make a bed up for you to aid your comfort?" Goldie replied heading for the bedroom so that Amélie couldn't see her grinning from her veiled insult masquerading as lighthearted humour. I had to suck my cheeks in order not to laugh, thankfully even if Amélie did understand Goldie's wit she didn't show it, instead she just nodded and waved her hand in acceptance.

Goldie returned from the bedroom and curtsied, "your room awaits my lady," she added tongue in cheek. Amélie tutted and disappeared into thin air amid a few moans and groans.

Eventually and suitably refreshed from her covert operation Amélie was ready to spill the beans. Goldie and I sat in deck chairs listening as she started by informing us how dangerous this had been for her and she could have got herself killed, but she did it for us. I do wonder exactly what planet she is on sometimes, is it that she forgets she is dead, is it that she refuses to accept it or maybe she is just irritatingly annoying as she knows it pushes our buttons. I could strangle her at times, anyway neither Goldie or I rose to it and she continued.

Amélie stood up and positioned herself cross-legged in front of us as if she was about to tell a small group of children a story. "We artists speak with words and without, we are nature's soul-restoration crew." I nodded as Goldie circled her hand as if to tell Amélie to get on with it. "Now then at great danger to myself I decided to go and look for the fisherman's boat, eventually I found it but I had to widen my search and go nearly to Nevis. The first time I found it, it was anchored just north of Charlestown, off of Pinney's Beach. It was pretty exposed and windy there with quite a swell. When I went back again it had been moved to Oualie Beach on the Northwest corner of the Island." She paused and adjusted her position as Goldie and I looked at each other, "Why Nevis?" I asked, Goldie shrugged her shoulders, our questions were brought to an abrupt halt as Amélie coughed. "Ahem, so I watched as these other boats came over, bobbing on the waves, in a sort of chaotic dance. They put boxes on the fishing boat and then left." "What time was this?" I asked her. "I don't know, I don't wear a watch, I am a ghost, remember." Hearing the frustration in my voice Goldie calmly asked, "Was it light or dark, day or night?"

Amélie thought for a moment before replying, "A bit of both, maybe evening?" Of course it was going to be a bit of both, why did we even pose that question, when Amélie was involved nothing was simple! "Now, then I hitched a ride on the faster boat and saw a bigger ship near to the harbour. I have to say it looked like it had blossomed right there on the ocean, with masts that stood tall with sails that were as pretty as any petals, bluish white in compliment to the sky and waves. The rest was all as solid as any oak of the land, warm browns that reminded me of Iberville. Her bows met the water with a regal dignity, as she bobbed up and down with the gentle tide." "Amélie, for goodness sake spare the artistic descriptions and get to the point." I really was beginning to get quite irked, this was hindering our investigation, we needed to be out there. "Détendez-vous," came her reply, "never mind relax, just get to the damn point" Goldie said. "I have nearly finished anyway, then I saw a bunch of pirate thieves, they had no code at all, no honour, just cold hearted thugs with swords and guns and a mafia boss that looked like a demon." "Really?" I asked at her dramatic descriptions, Amélie smiled and nodded.

She was infuriating, "I feel we need to investigate this for ourselves" I said turning to face Goldie who was already nodding in agreement. "Yep, this evening as it gets slightly dark Locked and Loaded will make their move." "No" we both said together as our pain in the you know what ghost was about to ask if she could come.

Amid annoying interruptions from Amélie, trying to tell us the best way forward we planned our mission with precision, we needed to find out more but without getting caught. We even went to Ziggy's bar in the hope he would lend us his boat, of course he was very obliging, anything to catch Mogsey's murderer. He was quite astounded that the boat had made its way to Nevis and slightly perturbed that we wouldn't let him come with us. Bless him, he was ready to shut the bar and motor us down there. Thankfully after an explanation along the lines of 'compromising our investigation' he relented and just gave us keys to the boat.

Phew, could you imagine if he had insisted on coming with us, shutting the bar would be an outrage and local gossip would mean half the Island would want to be involved, doesn't bare thinking about. We thanked Ziggy, promising to bring his boat back in one piece and then left calling into the minimart to pick up a few bits and pieces including wetsuits and spearguns, which neither of us owned anymore, we needed to prepare for any eventuality.

CHAPTER 31

So early evening arrived, we had planned and rehearsed for every eventuality, we had notified the Commissioner, who was out of town on some other function, no surprise there then!

We drove Goldie's truck to the beach and parked it out of sight, as we collected our backpacks and changed into the wetsuits, something in the near distance was waving frantically at us. Great Amélie, thank goodness it was only us that could see her, otherwise it would be a dead giveaway, if you pardon the pun!

 As we arrived next to her, I realised she had that damn locket around her neck. "How on earth did you get that, thought I had hidden it?" I uttered. "Not well enough for ghosts, remember I can secretly watch you and no you are not having it back" came her reply. Goldie rolled her eyes, "Suppose you are coming with us then?" She spoke softly this time as if she couldn't be bothered to argue anymore. "Yes, I am, you will need my help" Amélie replied very matter of fact.

We put our stuff into Ziggy's boat and started the engine, luckily both of us knew how to handle a small boat, our plan was to motor and then row once we neared Nevis so as not to draw attention to ourselves. Amélie was already ahead of us, having decided to show off and walk across the water. Well, that ended suddenly and quite dramatically as she began to sink. At first it was her feet disappearing beneath the calm sea, followed by her legs and her body. At first everything was serene until she realised what was happening and then it all became a bit loud and a bit splashy, waving her arms frantically about as she dipped below the waves and came up again in a dramatic fashion.

Why on earth can't this ghost get herself out of her own scrapes, suffice to say, we ended up having to scramble to rescue her. Goldie steering the boat whilst I managed to calmly coerce her into jumping as she landed head first into the boat in a dishevelled heap onto one of the backpacks. "How did you manage to swim whilst on surveillance, but not tonight?" I asked her. Amélie shrugged her shoulders commenting, "Look at me I am all wet, I could catch a chill and die." "You are dead, you muppet!" Goldie pushed her off the backpacks as Amélie started to unzip a few pockets to see inside. "Leave them" she snapped again.

Amélie looked at me, "What's inside?" she asked, "Just things we will need for our investigation." I replied as Goldie cut the engine. I removed the binoculars from the bag and caught sight of Mogsey's boat in the distance. I pointed towards it as Goldie picked up the oars. "We need to row the rest of the way and whisper from now on" she said. "Ok, not a problem!" Amélie whispered back, retrieving one of the oars from Goldie's hand and plunging it into the water. Goldie snatched it back as I came up with a novel plan. "Amélie, you sit at the front and be our look-out, Goldie and I will row." Amélie seemed extremely proud to be made the head hauncho! She sat at the front giving orders as we both took control of the oars and let the paddles sweep through the calm waters.

We reached the port side of the bow of Mogsey's boat, the plan was to stay out of sight of the harbour for now, whilst we investigated further. We tied onto the anchor buoy and hauled ourselves across from Ziggy's boat to Mogsey's leaving Amélie standing up as look out. She was quite unstable in her stance and complained that she could go over at anytime. Goldie and I chose to ignore her moaning.

The contents of Mogsey's boat was covered with a tarpaulin, we lifted it up and over, trying hard to keep our balance, only to reveal a number of large wooden boxes. We needed a closer inspection, so armed with a small crowbar we lifted the lids of a couple, nearly vomiting in the process. The smell was rancid, "Yuk, it smells like ancient cabbage!" Amelie remarked, I was inclined to agree with her, whatever was underneath the packing was not alcohol that was for sure. Across the top of the boxes, straw bales lay, by torchlight each strand had its own unique variation. As I moved it, I felt a roughness, a brittleness. I cut the twine holding the straw in place and a small plume of dust was emitted. It was then I touched something quite unexpected, a bit moist but certainly squishy. "Goldie, lower your torch, I need to see more." I whispered as she obeyed. We both retched at the sight, bovine eye balls, dead eyes staring into nothing, a few of them squished and leaking their jelly.

I retched again, "What on earth is it?" Goldie asked. I took a deep breath and picked one of the more squished ones up, peeling apart the eye slightly to reveal a chip of ever-cold ice, stubbornly resistant to all attempts to warm it. Goldie held it up closer to the torch, rubbing away the jelly substance. We both looked at each other astonished, before saying in unison "Diamonds."

This case was getting more and more confusing by the minute, was Mogsey killed for the alcohol, did he discover an illegal haul, is that why his boat was stolen, but what about the locket, what about Tilly? So many questions that we didn't have solutions too. At that very moment Amélie alerted us with her shouts "People coming right now."

We felt Mogsey's boat jolt as another boat bumped into the side of it, "Some look out you are Amélie, thanks so much for the warning" I whispered sarcastically as Goldie and I frantically replaced everything apart from the diamonds we had found and hid beneath the tarpaulin. There was a moment of extended silence, before a man's voice bellowed, "What the hell where did this boat come from? We need to deal with this immediately before the boss finds out." We tried to peer out as two of the men boarded Mogsey's boat and started the engine releasing it from its mooring. Gunshots echoed, ripping holes through Ziggy's boat, stealing away its very existence. The boat took on water at an alarming rate until finally, only the tip of the bow was above the waterline. Then that slipped away too taking Amélie with it. I am sure she could get herself out of that situation, she was a ghost after all!

Mogsey's boat was now under tow by the other boat, we could feel the wind gently gusting with the tempo of a fiddle, dancing with long and short bows, punctuated by a soulful silence, but propelling us onward. As we hid in the cramped space between the boxes, the old planks still retained the odour of the fish amid the nets bundled onto the deck, lovely.

Trying to peer out a bit more without being caught, all that was really visible was a blue boat rim a few inches above the water line and in the distance Amélie screaming for us not to leave her in the water as, now, she couldn't swim. "You would think she could transport herself to us wouldn't you?" Goldie whispered, I nodded, trying to plan our next move in my head. We tried to listen to the conversation between the people, but it was impossible, definitely male, but their words seem to tumble from their lips too fast for us to catch them.

Each word seemed to flow seamlessly into the next and was spoken so softly that it caressed the ears without transferring any meaning.

The boat's engine now slowed, we peered out as far as we dared, we were definitely now coming alongside a much larger boat, probably the yacht. Suddenly there was a jolt and a bit of a commotion, Goldie lifted the tarpaulin a bit more to see Amélie climbing aboard dripping wet and was keeping the crew busy by moving things around. Somehow she mastered command of Mogsey's boat in the hope that we could make our getaway, good thinking for a ghost.

Unfortunately the crew became a bit spooked as the boat jolted all over the place with no-one seemingly to be steering. "Montez rapidement dans le bateau et partez, je vais occuper ce lot pour l'instant, rapidement." Amélie screamed. We wanted to do exactly as she said but we were caught up in the heat of the moment so to speak, Its not every day you see a small frame of a woman taking on three muscular crew men.

It looked like they were fighting with themselves as it was only us that could see the ghostly encounter. One man threw up his forearms in self defence, but then his elbow came back down and caught his head, rolling him into the scuppers. The two other men rushed across to him as their wrists seem to twist back and over as they too were slammed onto the deck.

Amélie pounded on their foreheads several times as she screamed at us once more. "Montez dans le bateau, espèce d'idiots."

CHAPTER 32

It was now or never, we could continue to hide and quake with fear crouching underneath the covers or we could slink out whilst Amélie did her best to keep the crew occupied. So we took our chances, grabbed hold of one of the deck cleats, and made our way to the cabin to take control of the steering column, not an easy task against the boats unsteady sway.

Just as we thought we had made it, a voice bellowed at us. "Not so fast or I will shoot." We both turned remaining calm, now kneeling in the bottom of Mogsey's boat trying to keep our balance. Steadying myself, I assessed him as I reached behind me for a speargun. The man kept the gun pointed at the both of us, but we knew exactly what to do. Moving swiftly and confidently, I brought the gun around and fired, luckily the man was completely unprepared for such a manoeuvre as the spear brushed his arm. It gave me just that fraction of a second I needed to grab the barrel and twist the gun out of his hand and into my own. I held onto the gun firmly and pointed it at our opponent, roles reversed, that was easy, I thought to myself.

Goldie nudged me and nodded gesturing to look forwards, I wobbled a bit as I looked past the man. There she was, looking extremely different, but we recognised the voice, that could never be disguised. "Put the gun down Jasmine." She uttered, "Get them aboard quickly you fools." She said to the crew who were picking themselves up out of the hull. Great, now where was our ghost when we needed her most! "Tilly?" I said, "No speaking, get up the ladder and onto the yacht" she commanded.

As Goldie and I climbed the rope ladder onto the yacht, the adrenaline started to surge through me. My muscles felt stronger and I was more awake than I've ever been since Anegada, but this wasn't a situation we could easily run from, I think we were going to need help.

We grabbed the hand holds one by one and hauled ourselves up and over the rail of the yacht. This boat was enormous and very luxurious, now I am not good with lengths and widths but if I was to take a guess, I would say it was possibly about one hundred feet in length if not more.

The yacht was lit up like a fairground, if Tilly didn't want to be seen she was not doing a very good job. As we boarded we both checked out our surroundings as we had been taught when training. There was plenty of sleek and practical seating covered in Silvertex fabric, there was a huge platform at the front which I would have used it for sunbathing under different circumstances. We were marched into another huge room still at gun point. Possibly a lounge, but an entertainer's delight anyhow. More seating, impressive sound system, two big screen TV's, three refrigerators and four ovens. It looked like the seating also converted to a bed, meaning we could always extend our welcome to an overnight or weekend stay, I think not, we needed to get out of here quickly. "Sit down, the pair of you," she uttered and we obeyed.

Tilly walked over to us, her beauty was mind boggling, what had she done? She waltzed with an effortless saunter, the clicking of her heels added rhythm as her beautiful hazel eyes scanned the room with determination. Her curves were soft but with the muscles of a dancer. She had a beauty that made those billboard-princesses look as paper thin as they were, she was something robust and real. Then her eyes met ours, even more questions began to surface, how did she survive, how did she land on her feet yet again doing whatever it is she was doing, how did she get this yacht, did she steal the locket, did she kill Mogsey and steal his boat? So many mysteries!

My head began to hurt with all this turmoil inside, we needed answers. "We thought you were dead, bitch," Goldie uttered breaking the silence. "Take them away, put them downstairs and tie them up, I will deal with them tomorrow" she commanded. Two muscular crewmen appeared from behind us, one obeyed with a husky drawl, sauntering, every step he took was in slow motion, oozing a calmness. The other man was a clear head higher than most people I would consider tall but he isn't lanky though, there's bulk on him too as well as muscles, his strides carrying him further and faster than the first man.

Goldie and I were hauled to our feet and almost dragged down a narrow wooden spiral staircase into a below-decks cabin. I have to say, I couldn't think of a better place to be held captive if that's what has to happen.

This cabin was below the waterline with portholes on one side, sealed with heavy-duty glass. On the other side were panoramic windows from ceiling to deck, enjoying spectacular views of the underwater world and any sea creatures that might pass by. Otherwise apart from two large semicircular sofas and an open, and may I say empty, cocktail bar, it was pretty sparse. "We will deal with you tomorrow" one of the men uttered before closing and locking the door. Great, it was freezing cold, probably from the air conditioning as there was no real air here but we were still fairly warm from our wet suits.

Despite our new found predicament, we were not tied up or gagged and free to roam around which we did straight away looking for an escape route, there wasn't one! Our wet suits were beginning to itch, as I looked at Goldie, she had already peeled the neoprene off her top half to reveal her bikini, cold or no cold I needed to do the same.

Our backpacks had been left behind, so we had nothing to eat or drink and more importantly where was our ghost when we really needed her, she could help us escape, couldn't she? Goldie and I sat on the sofas bouncing ideas off of one another, trying to work out what was going on, funny really but we didn't actually feel very scared.

Just at that very moment something caught our eye as a strange looking mermaid slid down the side of one of the large windows. She was illuminated by some weird green light and was waving at us. Goldie and I looked at one another before announcing, Amélie. "Get in here now, we need you to help us," we uttered as loudly as we could but still trying not to be too loud in case we were heard by the crew. The glass was obviously too thick for her to hear through and instead she continued to pulsate down the glass like some sort of amoeba, arms and legs going everywhere.

Well, it was worth a try, if only we could figure out a way to get Amélie's help, why was she never around when we needed help the most? Suddenly the yacht seemed to pitch from side to side followed by a judder, then before our very eyes a green algae-like slime mould began to evolve from between the decking planks until it became a puddle. The puddle seemed to stick to the floor in one area before solidifying into a person, "Sorry it was my only way of getting in"Amélie said, brushing the green slime from a little black number she seemed to now be wearing. Well, at least she was here.

Goldie and I had decided that as there seemed to be no way out and Amélie had made it clear that she couldn't walk though metal doors or pick the lock, we would tackle the crew when they came back for us. Amélie could keep Tilly busy, then if we could evade the crew we could make our escape overboard and back to Ziggy's boat for our escape.

CHAPTER 33

Just then the door opened, neither Goldie or I had been aware that evening had turned into the following morning. "Eat this we will be back soon" we were told as a bowl of granola, some fruit and water were placed beside us. A good sign if they were feeding us, it meant Tilly needed us alive, maybe she had asked for ransom?

Amélie started to move into my cereal bowl with her physic powers, I quickly retaliated and moved it away from her sticky mitts, I needed to eat more than she needed to mess around. She glared at me, "Amélie, go and get some help, let anyone know where we are, go now, whilst Goldie and I figure out things." I spoke softly. "No, I will stay with you two, it's a nasty world out there, I could get into a serious situation or even worse end up dead." Amélie replied. In unison Goldie and I raised our voices, "You are dead!" Amélie no one can see you apart from us, go and get help now!" I repeated, Goldie raising her eyebrows to the ceiling once more in an exasperated fashion. "Ok, as I am dead and invisible, how do you propose I alert someone, dis moi ça." She uttered sarcastically, my god, she was infuriating. "Use your initiative, think of something!" Goldie shouted as the door opened once more. "Upstairs," came the tall mans voice.

Goldie and I did as we were told, leaving Amélie alone in the cabin, hopefully thinking about how she was going to raise the alarm and muttering something in French to herself. We were taken above deck to another large room which overlooked a huge sun deck, the yacht was moored at sea although you could see the harbour. If only we could overpower them, we could dive overboard and swim to shore, it wasn't far.

Tilly was sat on the sofa and immediately stood up as we entered the room, always was the domineering type. "Sit," she said, we obliged. She walked confidently across the floor, like a victor after a battle, until she stopped strutting and stood with her hand gently resting on her waist, her vision, piercing and cold falling on us. "Why are we here?" I asked trying to be just as confident. "To get what's coming to you, you killed Ed" she uttered very matter of fact. "Bitch," Goldie muttered under her breath as I nudged her. "We can't make sense of this, tell us please" Goldie uttered nodding downwards and gripping my hand. I hung my head low to look at her hand and realised she had a mobile phone on her now recording the conversation. Great work, but if I knew that earlier we could have phoned for help, although to be fair she probably had thought of it but had no reception.

I looked up and confidently asked, "Tilly we want answers, you owe us that much before you kill us." Goldie and I watched as Tilly thought briefly before replying "answers to what, I ask the questions here" "but do you, what the hell is going on, the least you could do is answer the questions, it's not like anyone will know apart from us is it? We can't exactly write them down. We watched her think again, all we needed to hope for now was that she didn't want to frisk us, hopefully she wasn't on the ball and would miss things.

She sat down across from us and made chilling eye contact. "Ok, go on then" she uttered. Goldie and I looked at one another, Goldie went first. "So in Anegada, you came after the four of us and despite our efforts to save you, we watched you drown, didn't we, how are you back from the dead?" Tilly nodded, "You would like to think so, I wanted revenge, you killed my Ed, in order to preempt you, I hid my diving gear in a nearby coral cave. All I then needed to do was flounder a bit, look like I was drowning and eventually dive for the last time, swim for my dive gear and then resurface further up the shoreline out of view from you."

My turn next, "The locket, how and why did you get it, and involve Mogsey in the process, we are assuming you killed him?" Tilly sighed, "You mean my locket?" At this moment in time we half expected Amélie to appear to dispute this, but she didn't, Tilly continued. "Ed gave the locket to me, he had removed the picture of his wife. I heard Iberville had been sold to you and what's his face." "Tim" I interjected as she continued, "the last time I saw the locket was at Iberville, I had spent a few nights there after he had bought it for you, I needed to find a way to get to you. Anyway, I found my locket, then it disappeared again, so I came back for it and had a snoop around one night when you weren't there."

"I knew you would discover the locket missing at some point but I needed you both away from Iberville so I could get to you. Mogsey's brother was part of my smuggling ring but he tried to get out so he was killed. Mogsey being Mogsey of course tried to save him and I managed to involve him as part of my plan. He stored liquor for me in his lock up. I needed to move that liquor so blackmailed him into letting me use his boat. He asked too many questions, all I needed was the boat, so he met his unfortunate demise, thats when I had the idea to put the locket in his hand, I could get it back later."

She held up the locket and it glinted in the light, of course, it was in my backpack. "I knew Mogsey would come to you both for help with his boat, then you would investigate his murder too. Eventually it would lead you to me." She smiled with a sinister look about her. "But we can still convict you, we have evidence at Mogsey's lock up." I beamed, at last we could get one over on her. Tilly stood up, "But for how long?" she uttered as she retrieved a mobile phone from her blouse pocket and dialled a number.

We looked across the water to the shore of St Kitts, as an explosion rented the air as if it was intent on shattering the universe by ripping apart every atom, sparks flew into the sky, tumbling upwards as if their destiny called. Mogsey's lock up was now a mountain of flames, the mesmerising black smoke billowing upwards amid the warming blue sky. We watched helpless as the flames had no culture, no pity, no mind, just consuming whatever it pleased. Its only criteria was take it and reduce to ash or something molten and foul.

All our evidence was alight and we could do nothing except watch as the acrid smell of smoke, even at this distance left a nasty sting in our noses. On a positive note, it would alert the authorities. Tilly turned to face us, an evil glint in her eyes, "Slaughter is Satan's laughter." She said. Tilly was now a lost cause, a far cry from the editor she once was. "What about the diamond smuggling?" I asked her, trying to seem indifferent at what she had just done. "I don't want to talk anymore, your time has come" she seemed slightly irritated, "You owe us this," Goldie piped in, we needed to gain ourselves a bit more time, just in case Amélie had gone for help. "Right, then you die." Goldie and I squirmed a little, pulling on our wetsuits, without causing anyone concern enough to move.

Tilly began, "Diamonds are famously easy to smuggle, the high value of smaller stones means resources worth thousands of dollars can be carried and concealed with ease compared to gun trafficking. Most of the diamonds I deal in are from Sierra Leone's informal diamond trade, to the point where they are unregistered. They are mined by children and families forced into slavery in the mine to make money. The diamonds are smuggled by my controlled armed groups, who take care of domestic transits personally. Many investors want diamonds without papers, when you have no papers you get a higher price for the diamonds." So this is how you have afforded this yacht and never been caught?" I asked as Tilly paused for breath.

She smiled, another condesceding sneer with a hint of maliciousness. "There are government monitoring officers who go to places looking for smugglers, if they catch you and you are found guilty, you pay a fine, but everything is negotiable. I don't get found, I am the predator at the top of the food chain if you like. I command who to slaughter, drug, recruit and trust. I am good at my job. As for the boat, I am baby sitting it for another mafia boss."

At this point, I am not sure whether Goldie still had her phone running or not, she had hidden it well in her wetsuit. "You are evil, what on earth turned you into this, another question," Tilly cut my sentence short. "Enough, no more questions, do you not think I know what you are doing? We need to go." Tilly nodded to the two men. Still no Amélie, time for Goldie and I to make our own move. I took the taller of the two men, whilst Goldie went for the more muscular, both of us performing the exact same manoeuvre in order to take them by surprise.

We each slapped our right palms down onto our opponent's face, as we had been taught, shattering their noses. Each of the men dropping their eyes to check on each other with equal measures of fury. Goldie yanked back with her left forearm, trying to snap the man's neck like a tree branch, she failed, he had anticipated it, so in the moments after landing on the floor he let his body relax. I had also managed to lay my opponent onto his hands and knees, as he scrambled to get up, I caught him, dragging him to his feet and turned my hip as he tried to knee me in the stomach. I pushed him away and hit him left, cross, straight right and he fell over onto the sofa.

Goldie and I glanced briefly at each other before taking another step forward, crowding them, slapping them once again across the face. It rocked them and they took a step back before steadying themselves, our final blow to make our get away was hitting them with our fists just under their ribs where the sternum ends. They both gasped and doubled over onto the ships steering wheel. "Enough, stand still or I will shoot you now." Tilly screamed, a gun in her hand aimed, loaded and ready to shoot at any given moment. There was no way she would miss us that was for sure. "Tie them up," she yelled throwing a rope to the nearest man, who reluctantly removed himself from the steering wheel and grabbed first my hands and then Goldie's. This wasn't in the plan!

CHAPTER 34

We were led off the yacht and bundled into the trunk of an awaiting car. Now something from our training came to mind; different types of rope require different methods of escape. The rope our hands were tied with was plain rope, so it needed to have a loose knot. We also resisted letting our captors tie us as tightly as possible by, holding our knuckles from both hands together, and pulling our hands in towards our chest, it actually looks like we are cooperating, but in actual fact it creates a gap between our wrists hopefully to aid our escape later.

 As Goldie and I were unceremoniously bundled into the boot of a car, we glanced quickly for any boot release we could reach on the inside. Typical, not one, any competent killer will have thought of this. The boot was closed and the car began to move as Goldie and I were squashed still trying to remain calm and conserve air. Even if we had been able to get out of this moving car, we would have had to throw ourselves out, get hurt, find that there's no one around to help and ultimately get chased by the men and thrown back in the car, so not a great move.

After what seemed an age but wasn't, the car came to a halt and the boot was opened. "Get them out" Tilly bellowed at the two men still nursing bloody hands and faces. Goldie and I looked around, taking in our surroundings. "Move" Tilly commanded again poking me in the back with her gun. I nodded to Goldie who started walking behind one of the men. There was a yellow cemented wall and we turned right onto a dirt track. At first we seemed to follow an old railway line but when that dried up we were led through a burned out cane field and then followed a creek bed upstream. After about a 10 minute hike we climbed down a relatively steep bank into a cave.

The cave or 'Bat Cave' as it is affectionately known locally, is actually an old terras pit from colonial times where a sort of volcanic sand was mined and used to make mortar for stone walls and buildings. Mixed with lime made from burnt shells or coral and water, it formed a durable cement and was in use all over Nevis. Nowadays the cave is home to a few bats hanging from its ceiling and a few sheep skeletons embedded in the small crevices at the back of the cave, they used to come and graze on the rich seaweed and then found they couldn't get out. The cave looks out across the water and is pounded by waves in very strong winds, sometimes it has been known to flood.

We were ushered just inside the cave, far enough to be out of sight but not far enough to be out of danger. As we looked around for an escape route, Goldie and I were tied to a metal ring hanging out of one of the rocks. Our hands were untied and then retied, tighter this time, despite us trying to remain calm and not tense up, hopefully we would still have enough slack to get ourselves out. We both concentrated on how the rope was being tied, to give us another advantage. Our hands were pulled behind our backs and the rope was looped through the ring, several times, I think, before being tied in a figure of eight pattern and then wrapped between our wrists so our hands can't be wriggled free. It was then secured with a knot below our thumb joints out of reach of our fingers.

This was going to take some doing, but this was the whole point, we were here to meet our demise. "Lets get out of here" Tilly uttered, lowering her gun and placing it back in her pocket, she knew she was safe now, we couldn't do anything. Her crew obeyed orders instantly and withdrew as her passing words echoed around the cave. "Its your turn now, may you die with your conscience, see what it feels like, drowning is a bitch of a way to go!" With that we were alone.

Goldie and I looked at each other, the same feeling entering our minds, we were going to die if we didn't get out of here. Goldie peered out, "Bad weather is on the way, we need to do something fast." I nodded but also asked "how do you know?" Goldie replied" it's the air pressure, look at the smoke from Mogsey's lock up, before it was spiralling into the air, now it is spiralling back down around the fire, which means the air pressure is low." I never knew she was a meteorologist as well.

We did need to get out of here very soon. We both wriggled around, trying to get ourselves into positions we had never tried in order to loosen the ropes, it didn't work. There wasn't even enough slack for us to try and get back to back to unpick each others rope knots. We were only in water shoes and had nothing sharp. We tried to move nearer the rock, we just needed to find a sharp bit to cut the rope, but even that was impossible, the rope was just too tight to permit any movement.

Then a rumbling sound echoed and began to growl, like a freight train hurtling through a tunnel. The entire cave felt like it was shaking in an earthquake. This was it, how were we going to get out alive? Then as if by some divine intervention Amélie appeared, thank goodness. "Amélie," with both shouted, relief in our voices, "Quickly untie us, we haven't got long." I shouted and the echo rang around the cave. Amélie's face was one of perfect misery, her hands and face blackened amid tracks of dried tears. "What happened to you?" Goldie asked as Amélie positioned herself behind us to untie the ropes. "I was in your friends lock up, when it exploded, nearly killed me." Goldie and I looked at one another and rolled our eyes. "Oh, Tim and Leroy are back, she commented casually" "Did you get help?" I asked. "I think so" came her reply. "What do you mean you think so?" Goldie asked as Amélie peered over our shoulders, Its not easy to get help when you are invisible, but the last time I saw them, they were at your truck" she nodded at Goldie. "Zigglet or whatever his name is, told them you had gone to Nevis. I left a bat in your truck, so when they open it, they will hopefully put two and two together." Not bad going for an irritating ghost I must say, let's hope that was enough for them, it should be, spies are used to fathoming things out on minimal clues.

CHAPTER 35

The rumbling sound returned echoing for longer this time, followed by a thunder as a wave pulsed, roaring and splashing into the cave. "Hurry up Amélie." I shouted intensely." "I'm trying my best but I can't undo the knot, I am going to get wet" she moaned "you and us both, hurry up" Goldie insisted.

Just in the nick of time, Amélie flew backwards through the rock as the ropes came free. A wave pulsed onto the rocks and through the cave before receding, before we had chance another wave hit, bursting through cave with such force that we were swept off the rocks and into the sea. A great mountain of water showing us its anger and turbulence, unforgiving. Every one of our senses is maxed out, every muscle in our bodies already working beyond normal capacity with no end in sight, the waves crashing like a coiffured fifties hair do, over pronounced in their arches. "Goldie, grab onto a rock, grab onto a rock." I screamed at her, hoping she could hear me over the thunderous noise of the waves.

I tried to grab hold but there was nothing there, the water had slurped me off the rocks and was forcing me under. The salt stung my eyes, there was no safety. The waves spat me up for a moment, I screamed for Goldie, but couldn't see her, I screamed again this time for help. I shut my burning eyes and tried to swim, battling the warm water with a breaststroke, but then realised that the sea had sucked me even further out.

The next time my head bobbed beneath the waves I was still not too worried, I have after all dived before and I am not too scared of a little water over my head, each time I fall beneath the waves I still expect to come back up, and I do, but each chance to breathe becomes further apart, each breath I take seems less than the last. The trouble is, after only a few seconds I feel like I am sinking again, my legs are feeing tired and this time, I am struggling to come back up towards the sun-speckled surface of the waves. I managed to find my super human power once more as I broke the surface again, gulping at the summer air and then with barely a splash I was under again.

This time I sank faster and the shear panic had my heart hammering against my ribs. Nobody is looking, no one has seen me or Goldie. It's coming to the point when I can no longer hold my breath, the cold water rushes in and all illusions of surviving are going. Soon the oxygen deprivation will take away my thoughts and I will be lost at sea, my beloved Tim all alone to deal with the consequences. I have held my breath before, but this isn't like that, it is like having a gun to my head and being told not to let my heart beat, of course it will beat and just like my heart must go on, my lungs will take in what ever is there, air or water it doesn't matter. In that moment that the coolness rushes in I know I am about to die, float like the sea weed, nothing more than flesh and bones ready to decay in the currents. Before I go under that final time I know I have been kissed by the sun for the last time.

The current took me down as I strained for the light that began to dim above my head. I moved my arms like I was trying to climb, but it was just water around me, washing around my body preventing any access to precious air. My brain is in full panic, fear and then more panic. I thought I was about to become dead. As the sunlight got further away, my hair began to float upwards, it felt like seaweed rising, rippling in the currents. My movements became completely uncoordinated, just clawing through the thin liquid, from my lips came an explosion of air bubbles, moving away from me at a peculiar angle.

I realised that I wasn't facing upwards, instead struggling perpendicular to the surface, my thoughts becoming groggy, as my struggling limbs slowed down. I was floating in the current like a doll. At that moment I felt something clasp onto my wrist with a slight awareness that I am being towed upwards to the daylight above, I slowly opened my eyes, that's when I realised that Tim's hand had found my arm and he was pulling me upwards to safety.

I felt my head come out of the water, sensed the warmth of the sun and the feeling of still being dragged. Then I opened my eyes once more as I felt a warm soft bed beneath me, I must have shut my eyes again. Apparently after laying me on the sandy shore, Tim performed artificial resuscitation on me, I had swallowed a lot of the salty sea water. The next thing I remember is being rolled onto my side as I coughed out the water.

By now, I was awake, shaking, slightly uncoordinated in my movements looking at Tim, my hero, " Jasmine, Jaz, are you all right?" Tim asked anxiously as he crouched next to me. I grimaced before howling in pain, gesturing to my legs that were cramping. "Shh, my darling, it is ok, you are fine now, here, let me ease your pain." Tim uttered rubbing my numbed legs, until gradually, I stopped groaning my face visibly relaxed. "Goldie, where is Goldie?" "Shh, she is fine, she is with Leroy just a little further up the beach." Tims voice was so calming.

I managed to sit up, only to see a small crowd of locals had gathered, concerned for us, curious as to what had happened. I didn't care about them, I just wanted to make sure Goldie was really alive. "I need to see her," I uttered struggling to stand. "Jaz, she is fine, just rest, we need to get you to a medical centre." Tim replied. "No, no I am fine, no hospitals, I just want to see Goldie and then you take me home." I heard some muttering and then Tim handed me his mobile, "Here," he said. I took the phone from him, "Hello," I managed to say, my brain feeling slightly befuddled. "Jaz, thank god, we are both ok," came Goldie's voice at the other end of the phone. I felt myself relax knowing that we had both survived to tell another tale, with that in mind my stomach lurched and gurgled before vomiting up more sea water. I tried to raise my heavy eyelids half way only for them to fall shut, I don't remember anything else, except for hearing Tim say to someone, "this ends now." At that moment in time, I really couldn't have cared any less, I was just comforted that both Goldie and I were safe, we were with Tim and Leroy and nothing could happen now.

CHAPTER 36

As Goldie and I rested back at Iberville, well as much as you can with all the goings on DIY wise. Leroy and Tim disappeared allegedly to Ziggy's bar. However knowing these two as we do, they would be nowhere near that vicinity as that was later confirmed.

In fact Tim and Leroy really did feel that enough was enough and went back to Nevis in search of Tilly and the yacht we were held against our will on. However, despite an extensive search they returned to St Kitts completely empty handed, Tilly and the yacht had completely vanished into thin air.

Being in the spy world neither Tim or Leroy were going to give up lightly, so went to the expense of hiring a helicopter with infra red cameras, letting it swoop like a bird over the area and beyond in search of our vanishing cartel, but alas they still drew a blank. On questioning the locals, no one admitted to seeing or hearing anything, even the harbour masters seemed to have no idea of what Tim and Leroy were on about. Odd as the yacht had been moored to the harbour side whilst it took on its illegal cargo, had she warned them off?

Despite their best efforts, bless them, there was absolutely no trace of the ship ever being docked, setting sail or arriving anywhere else. Does this mean the yacht has been lost at sea with its crew, surely someone must know something? I guess lost is a matter of perspective, Tilly was probably enjoying life where ever she was right now.

Tim told us that there is something ghoulishly fascinating about a ships mysterious disappearance, I can sort of see his point, but I suppose the yacht and its crews true fate will never be known especially if Tilly was still involved with the mafia. The mafia is a twisted society that will always look after its own, so Tilly could be anywhere by now.

A good while later, Goldie and I had recovered from our ordeal enough to write up our statements and given a verbal account of proceedings to the commissioner. Tim and Leroy handed over the search for Tilly to the CIA and had actually solved two more reasonably short investigations. Tilly was still at large but we had found enough evidence to narrow down the search area for the CIA. Amélie was pleased that she had managed to retrieve her locket and had become a much more tolerable ghost. Even Tim was impressed that she managed to leave clues to our whereabouts whilst being invisible. He joked that she should become a spy, so many a day she was sat next to the new swimming pool that used to be the orangery, reading up on spy tactics. It was quite odd seeing a book in mid air, even Tim felt unnerved by it, but it kept her quiet and out of harms way.

Goldie and Leroy had just about finished their home improvements with the shack, they had done a fantastic job, extending it to double its size by buying up the abandoned land next door to it. Iberville had now been transformed into the most luxurious mansion, I won't bore you with all the details but suffice to say, it has lavish interiors, our inspirations taken from international architecture, famous monuments, and trending decor styles. From the art nooks, rounded corners, crown mouldings, and archways installed in just the right places giving Iberville a unique touch. It has spacious rooms, open-viewing areas, balcony lawns, and so much more that I could ever wish for, the guys helped Tim and I carefully design and craft Iberville which has given it a modern but historical look.

My kitchen is so large, with top-class appliances, feature double ovens, heating drawers, island sinks, washers, too much to mention. We had to buy more furniture for the house including fancy lamps and LED TV's on each floor. We have even put air conditioning in every room.

Tim being security conscious has put in state of the art security features. I find it a bit of a hindrance, but Tim assures me you can never have too many smart locks, key codes, CCTV cameras, safety alarms, etc. The outhouses have also been transformed completely into idilic little cottages that the guys who work in the rum distillery live in with their families.

Enough about the house, the rum distillery has also been transformed, even Goldie, myself and Leroy have got involved with Tim. Well, we couldn't let him run with all the decisions could we? In fact our distillery has become known around the Caribbean Islands for its artisanal rum and unique, hand-painted bottle designs. We not only produce and sell but we now run tours around the distillery explaining about the molasses, fermentation, and distillation processes, sharing the step-by-step process and ingredients used in creating our famous rum. I quite enjoy being one of the guides, I get to wear a badge and a t-shirt as well!

After the tour, we let you taste our exclusive rum and even go as far as running workshops on some afternoons so that our visitors can learn how to craft their own cocktails.

Anyway enough of the boring stuff, Tim and I decided to hold a party for everyone, and when I say everyone, thats exactly what I mean, all those that work here now, have worked on the project and everyone who lives on the Island of St Kitts. Tim and I worked so hard on the preparation. It was going to be a masked ball and this was going to be one hell of a night! I only had to deal with a couple of incidents involving

Amélie, but I have to say on both occasions she was only trying to help.

The first incident involved the delivery of some fresh produce, when she felt that Guerdy had short-changed me, during the delivery. This resulted in a slight altercation between him and I when she let the air out of his tyres, but was soon resolved. The second was when she accidentally sat on a cake I had just made when she needed to think! I had asked her advice about decorations, so I had to start again but alls well that ends well I suppose.

After so much stress and frantic activity, the night of the party arrived. Our guests arrived by the dozen, each one wearing a mask decorated in gold or silver colours complementing their best party wear. The moon provided a natural disco ball, illuminating Iberville. Some of the workers living on site offered greetings to those coming up the steps through the tunnel of fairy lights that added a little extra colour. A sweet melody drifted through the bustling atmosphere as I weaved my way amongst the guests and champagne bearing waiters we had hired. I managed to save a silver tray adorned with various buffet foods just before it crashed into the wall. No one seemed to notice, "Let me take that, where do you think you are going with it?" I asked Amélie. "comment sais-tu que c'est moi? je porte un masque" came her reply. "I know it's you, because despite the mask and lovely red dress, sadly I am the only one that can see you.

With my question not answered I replaced the silver tray firmly back on the table for all to enjoy. A collection of violinists, harp players and pianists were playing some form of classical Caribbean music which Tim had asked for, it was lovely I stood idle by the door for a few minutes, listening, feeling the changes in the music and the stories it told. The energy levels were high and everyone was ready to party all night long. Thats exactly what we all did do, a good time was had by all, with memories we can share and keep.

CHAPTER 37

The following morning, I opened my eyes to the dimly lit room, neither of us had made it across to the window to open the curtains. I put my hand out to reach for the clock, but clumsily I knocked it on the floor, rousing Tim, one look at him tells me that his head is hurting just as bad. I squinted, my dry mouth felt sticky with thick saliva as I groaned before retreating back under the covers.

The aching in my skull ebbed and flowed like a cold tide, yet the pain remained constant, I understand why they call it a hangover, it feels as if the blackest of clouds are over my head with no intention of clearing.

By lunchtime, Tim and I were just about ready to surface, good job really as Goodies' dulcet tones echoed up the spiral staircase, bouncing, full of beans, How could she not feel the effects, she drank just as much as me. Tim and I made ourselves respectable and joined her and Leroy downstairs.

We had forgotten that we had invited them over to reveal a secret that we had found under a large cabinet during the renovation work. Amélie took great pride in coming with us alerting us to the fact that this had always been there, but she never told Ed about it, it was her secret.

Anyway after removing the cabinet, we discovered a hatch covering stairway down into what we thought was a cellar. Tim put on his backpack loaded with the staff's wages for the week so he could go straight on to them after our search. We all excitedly descended down the staircase with our torches, Amélie in the lead. Once below the house, a huge cellar widened out with a door at the end. It wasn't locked so we went through to investigate, finding ourselves in a long tunnel. It was hard to tell how far we walked, but it must have been at least a full five minutes before abruptly the tunnel lost its brickwork and became a cave with stone steps swirling upwards. At some point in the proceedings Amélie must have become bored as once again she had done her famous disappearing act.

We ascended to find ourselves just a few feet away from the grinding house. The exit was covered in ivy and other shrubs and was so well concealed that Tim and I had never noticed its existence. Just when you think you know Iberville, it reveals something else to you.

As we all stood above ground once more, we realised there was a terrible commotion coming from the grinding house. Goldie and Leroy decided to make a quick getaway leaving Tim and I to hurry over to see what it was all about and give out the weeks wages. As we approached, the screams and shouts rose in intensity, this was not going to be an ordinary disagreement between staff so we quickened our pace to deal with this urgent situation.

When we arrived, we couldn't believe our eyes, there was Tilly in broad daylight dancing around as if she was having some type of fit. The guys that were working in the grinding house were trying to catch her but at their every move she resisted. Tim went forward to try and catch hold of her, but as he did she escaped from his grasp and climbed up onto the bales of sugar cane that were still waiting to be fed into the grinding wheel.

She was ducking and diving, twisting and turning, screaming and shouting obscenities as I moved forward to be nearer to try to help Tim remove her from the bales of sugar cane. I caught sight of Amélie punching and kicking her as hard as she could, quite impressive for a ghost! "Stop Amélie, stop it right now." I yelled, everyone looked at me as if I had gone completely mad. "Is she here?" Tim asked me, I nodded and pointed towards her ghostly figure now climbing off of Tilly's back, a complete waste of time as it was only me and Tilly who could see her. "Get away, get off, you monstrous old hag, Jaz, get her off of me" screamed Tilly looking over in my direction with her hardened eyes.

I put my hands to my mouth and gasped as with one final swoop, Amélie punched Tilly in the stomach with so much force that she lost her footing and fell backwards onto the threshing machine, she screamed with such a raw intensity, completely primal, a desperation from the place or terror she was now in, her mind lost in absolute fear. "Shut it down, shut it down, NOW." Tim yelled as Elian one of the guys in the grinding house raced to the emergency shut-down button, whilst Vincent tried to help Tim in a desperate attempt to save Tilly before she reached the wheel.

It was all in vain as the blades on the wheel had already caught her, they were sharp enough to cut flesh meeting absolutely no resistance. All we could do was watch her struggle and hear her hysterical shouts which turned to a gentle moan and then became a deathly silence as her body was crushed by the rollers. A fountain of red coloured the machine, its ebb and flow in time with a terrified failing heart, killing her all the faster. We stood watching as if we couldn't hear her screams of pain, as if it were a silent theatre production of no importance. We never moved at all until she had bled out, her red blood mingled with the gravel and sugar cane.

It was the actual hook on the machine which had done more damage than the blades, the sharp steel end had hooked into her neck and pulled out her carotid, ripping it in two, letting her blood pour as easily as water from a garden hose.

It had all been so silly, if only she hadn't tried to resist us, if only I had managed to control Amélie, the end may have been different. Tim looked at me and seeing the horror on my face uttered, "I had to try a rescue... if you don't try, then who are you? Where is your hero's heart?" He was right, she should not have been allowed to die that way.

Amélie stood on the sugar cane bale looking down, not a drop of blood on her. I hadn't seen her looking so pleased with herself for a long while, just a demon of self doubt troubling her ghost like form. Yet in its place had come a confidence that elevated her and had taken her to a happier place so that she could now rest. "What have you done?" I shouted as she jumped off the bale at the same time as Tilly's decapitated head plopped into one of the hessian raw waste bags.

"Je suis la meilleure hit lady" she renounced joyously, she hadn't had to care about money or killing evil bastards as she put it since she became a ghost. Nor could she ever be found out or punished, that said she could still get others into trouble for her misdemeanours. "It was a game of Russian Roulette, she took a chance and she got what she deserved" she said in her French American accent.

Tim was trying to clear up the mess as the rest of the workers had recoiled, scared they could be next, yet at the same time thinking how this grisly murder might be more lucrative for them. I am sure we needed to help them forget this incident very quickly, a bribe usually did the trick, if not, we could be in a lot of trouble. "Jaz, get Leroy on the mobile and tell him to come straight over, as for your ghost, do whatever you do to banish her, she is a pain in the…. "Cul," Amélie finished the sentence for him, sticking her tongue out at him. "He can't see you," I said, "Jaz, get her out of here, now" came Tim's angry insistent reply, "OK, ok, I know when I'm not wanted," she said and with that she walked through the wall of the grinding house and disappeared out of sight.

I rang Leroy and explained that he needed to come straight away, I couldn't give a synopsis on the phone, except to say Tilly. He was out the door and on the way as soon as he heard her name. I walked to where Tim was, "Stay away Jaz, it's not a pretty sight." "It's ok I want to help," I replied, "what do you want me to do?" Just then Leroy arrived with Goldie in tow. "Christ wah ah mess, Whappen? as she put her arm on my shoulder, "I have had enough French spoken at me, so no more Patois for now, let's just speak English." "Agreed." Leroy said winking at her.

As Tim explained to Leroy what had happened, they quickly came up with a plan. "Ladies get some cloths and the hose" Leroy uttered, we did as we were told. Tim then gave us instructions to move the sugar cane bales that were clean, putting them outside the grinding house, hose down everything else and try to put the hosed down cane into bags which we were to then place at the side. Meanwhile, Leroy and Tim would dispose of Tilly's body in a decent way.

We all set too with our tasks, as the men cleared away bits of Tilly and removed her for a secret decent burial somewhere in the grounds of Iberville, we went into tornado mode, cleaning and clearing, it seemed to us take ages. At some point in the proceedings Amélie reappeared and propped herself up against the wall. "You could help." Goldie said, slightly irked by her, "I could, but I don't get my hands dirty, I have people to do that!". I still had the hose in my hand, so turned it on full pelt and aimed it straight at her, God she knew how to make people angry. Unfortunately, as ghosts can choose to disappear at the most opportune moments, she did and instead Tim was blasted with the full force of the hose.

He was even less impressed, "What the hell are you doing?" he shouted as I quickly realised and turned off the hose, grinning at my completely sodden man.

Despite the grisly murder that had just occurred, we all seemed to see the funny side of things and burst into laughter. I turned around to walk back to the grinding machine and as I did I felt the full force of the water from the hose on my back, I spun round to accuse Goldie of foul play, only to find it was Tim. A water fight was not supposed to be the order of the day if we were to get this mess cleaned up, but it was our release you see.

Leroy surveyed the area, "I suspect the workers have gone back to their cottages to get changed and gossip, so we won't have much longer before they return. Lets leave larking around for now and get the job at hand finished." That was the reality check we needed as we finished up cleaning and clearing."Right the next plan is when Vincent, Neo, Elian and Anton arrive back, nothing happened here, it has all been imagined." Tim said, "Ok, but what about the blood on their clothes and Vincent trying to help you?' Goldie asked, having had the accounts relaid to her, "It was a chicken," I replied instantly, "good call." Tim said, they are not that clever that we can't convince them and a bonus in their wages will help. "Absolutely, you can say they have increased their production recently, so you have sold more rum, they won't know any differently" Leroy said just in the nick of time as the four men arrived back.

As they entered the barn, Leroy started a loud conversation with Tim, "So we just thought we would come over and let you be the first to hear the news…" The workers scratched their heads and looked completely bamboozled, "There you are, we have bought your wages." I said. Vincent the foreman, shook my hand as he always did and handed the packets to his three colleagues.

Anton, who I don't think I had ever heard speak uttered, "Er, where's the body, missy?" "Body?" Tim asked breaking off his conversation with Leroy. "Yes, there was blood all spurting out," Neo replied." "No, gentlemen it was a chicken, don't you remember, Vincent, you saw that when you tried to help Tim didn't you?" I said with a clarity to my voice. Vincent thought for a moment, removed his hat from his head and then put it back on again, "It did squawk a lot, is it proper dead?" "Yes," I replied. "Back to work then, otherwise we get no good money," was all Vincent said, before they returned back to what they were doing without any further questions, I never thought it would be this easy. They were good guys, they trusted us.

CHAPTER 38

As we all left the distillery area and walked back towards the house, I noticed Amélie walking back and forth at the entrance to the walled garden. "Tim, I will meet you inside, there is something I need to do. "Your Ghost?" he asked, raising his eyebrows at Leroy, I nodded. "I'm coming with you," announced Goldie.

Amélie spotted us as we approached and waved. "All sorted then?" she shouted. "What are you up to now?" I asked her as we arrived beside her, "You sound cross." I sighed," not cross Amélie, just, well, I'm not sure what the word is for it, sometimes there are better ways, that's all." "What are you wearing?" Goldie asked her, "Ma robe du soir, Je vais vous laisser tous les deux maintenant et dormir pour toujours plus." came her reply. I sighed again, "sorry, I know, I know, in English please" she joked and then repeated what she had just said. "My nightdress, I am going to leave you both now and sleep forever more.

I stared at her, "You are not, you caused this mess, I need you around in case things turn nasty, what if the authorities find out and come after Tim and me?" God, she could be so annoying at times, but I suppose annoyance is in the eye of the beholder, I should respond with a calmness instead of being reactive, that said, we all have limits.

Amélie smiled, "Nothing will happen, they are spies and can take care of themselves and everyone else ten times over, no one has seen Tilly, apart from us, so she will just remain on the run forever. Besides, because I am now at peace, my powers have gone, look." She went to poke the two of us, she was right, instead of the irritating prod that we never seemed to be able to evade, her boney fingers went straight through us.

I jumped, gosh, "You see I am really dead, now a proper ghost, so it is time to say farewell and move on, I will travel to heaven and be with my mother again." She spoke softly her eyes welling up as she did so. I suppose she did just have things to finish before passing on, and her need to do it was so great that the creator had given her a chance. Thus she was alive and dead, perhaps what some would call an angel.

Before I could ask her how she was going to go, Amélie cast her eyes around and inhaled the air as if she'd risen from the deep ocean, "Mmhm, cinnamon buns fresh from the oven," she announced, Goldie and I sniffed but all we could sense was fresh air, slightly sweet and floral. "My mother used to bake them after church, she's calling me, I can see her warm outstretched arms." So this was her heaven, baking cinnamon buns with her mother, not everyone's idea of heaven perhaps, but it was certainly hers. She turned to go, but paused, somehow knowing that Goldie was about to say something. "I'm going to have a baby," Goldie announced, "I know, look after your little one when she is born, you can call her after me if you like" Amélie uttered, but that fell on deaf ears.

"Congratulations Goldie," I said with a warm glowing feeling inside of me and then hugged her as if she was my favourite teddy bear. "I have news too." I said, "Are you?" "Yes, I am." came my reply. Goldie squealed. "This is so exciting, both of you will make the best mothers, Jaz, don't call your little boy Edward, it's a shame I won't be able to hold them but I will always be with you" Amélie said smiling. How did she know what we would have, even we didn't know I thought to myself. As she walked through the bricks of the walled garden never to be seen again, she uttered, "Merci de m'avoir aidé à reposer mes démons, Rappelez-vous que chaque meurtre est la fin d'une histoire, pourtant tant d'histoires en font le début.

Translated into English, what she said was, Thankyou for helping me lay my demons to rest. Remember every murder is the end of a story, yet so many tales take it as their start. With that she was gone and Goldie and I were left alone in our embrace and happiness.

Books by Vanessa Wrixon

Book Trilogy

Iberville
Book One
Iberville is the first book in a murder mystery series. Small time English Journalist Jasmine Tormolis lands herself a new job in the Caribbean. From there on in, her life takes some twists and turns as she and a local fishermen discover a woman's body washed up on the beach. Despite the Authorities corruption and fraud, Jaz decides to do her own investigative work, which lands her in deep water and leads to a kidnapping and the murder of two friends.

Temptation
Book Two
Continues to follow Jasmine Tormolis, but now as the boss of the Alise newspaper. Jaz and one of her reporters land themselves in hot water once more, when they are offered a chance holiday to another Caribbean Island. Here they try to become helpful accomplishes to a couple of secret agents they meet. Once again they find themselves being hunted down for revenge until their killers are killed or are they?

Haunted
Book Three
Jasmine Meyers formally Tormolis, now resides at Iberville with her new husband. Jaz and her reporter friend Goldie remain inseparable and help each other renovating their new abodes. Both try their hand at detective work, but it's not as easy as it looks. Lady Amelie Wrexham, having once owned Iberville reappears as a

ghost, trying to perfect the art of haunting. However, failure to do this effectively gives her a chance opportunity to help Jaz and Goldie catch a murderer and lay the Iberville demons to rest once and for all. Of course, this is not without problems when ghost thinks they can help.

Other Books by Vanessa Wrixon

Dark Nights
Camille Lavigne a French teacher at a secondary school, has arrived in England after a messy breakup. She finds her job frustrating to say the least. She becomes embroiled with a handsome man twelve years her junior, but despite a passionate steamy relationship, she is unaware of his dealings with the underworld and becomes the prime suspect in his murder, needing the help of her ex-husband to bail her out.

Sowing the seed
Petra Defeu is on a stakeout with her colleague. Having just moved into the area as a new detective, she hasn't quite got the measure of how things work and her colleagues can't yet get a measure of her. When she gets home from work one evening, her house has been burgled and there is a dead man in her kitchen. She then has to prove her innocence in a race against time before her colleagues or ruthless conspirators catch up with her.

Printed in Great Britain
by Amazon